Hawks of Autumn

Center Point
Large Print

Also by Wayne C. Lee and available from
Center Point Large Print:

Devil Wire
Showdown at Julesburg Station

Hawks of Autumn

Wayne C. Lee

CENTER POINT LARGE PRINT
THORNDIKE, MAINE

This Center Point Large Print edition
is published in the year 2024 by arrangement with
Golden West Inc.

First US edition: Avalon Books

The text of this Large Print edition is unabridged.
In other aspects, this book may vary
from the original edition.
Printed in the United States of America
on permanent paper sourced using
environmentally responsible foresting methods.
Set in 16-point Times New Roman type.

ISBN 979-8-89164-210-2 (hardcover)
ISBN 979-8-89164-214-0 (paperback)

The Library of Congress has cataloged this record
under Library of Congress Control Number: 2024933892

I

Clint Webb reined up just below the brow of the little hill, halting the four men behind him. Trouble could be waiting just over the knoll.

"Getting close?" Bruce Brill asked.

Webb nodded. Brill was the oldest of the four old men following Webb, but he was ready for a fight if it came to that and so were the rest of the men. Ace Gilmore and Lon Fleming were sixty years old, two years younger than Brill. Jay Oldham was the youngster of the quartet at fifty-nine.

"Before we go over this ridge, we'd better know what's waiting for us," Webb said. "They wanted this ranch so bad they killed to get it. They'll surely fight to keep it."

"It's not their ranch," Gilmore growled, "no matter what they did to get it."

"Let me check," Webb said.

He dismounted and moved up the side of the knoll. This was the only rise near the ranch buildings. The buildings were out on the Nebraska bottomland that reached back toward the sandhills from the Platte River. Webb had deliberately led the four men up here to keep their approach hidden from anyone who might be at the ranch.

As he neared the crest of the knoll, he lifted his head enough to peer over. The buildings were two hundred yards away. As he had anticipated, their ranch was occupied. A couple of horses stood at the hitchrack. He couldn't see much of the corral beside the barn, but he did see some horses in the corner that was visible to him. Apparently there were several people at the ranch, some of them staying permanently.

Sliding back down the hill, Clint got to his feet and faced the four men. "We've got trouble," he said. "There are several people down there."

"It's our ranch house, ain't it?" Brill asked.

Webb nodded. "It's ours but, like the saying goes, possession is nine-tenths of the law."

"Then we'll possess it," Gilmore said emphatically.

Webb thought he'd be just the man to do his part in possessing it. Ace Gilmore was big, over six feet tall and weighing more than two hundred pounds. His sharp black eyes could penetrate steel, Webb thought. They were the eyes of a gambler, which Gilmore had been. Never married, Gilmore had no family to leave if this venture claimed his life.

"Let's rush them," Bruce Brill said.

Webb looked at the oldest member of the group. Brill was the only one who really understood what it meant to operate a ranch. He'd been a cowboy most of his life and longed to own an interest in a ranch. This was his chance. His wife had died two years ago and he had no children. If he didn't live through this, nobody would mourn him.

"No sense in getting killed if we can help it," Webb warned. "Remember, they killed my pa and ma to get this ranch. They won't bat an eye if they have to kill again to hold it."

"They ought to spend some time in prison," Jay Oldham growled.

Oldham would know about that, Webb thought. He'd spent several years behind bars. His wife had left him when he went to prison for cattle rustling and now he had nothing to live for; at least, that was what he said. This venture was made for him.

"Let's plan our move," Lon Fleming said. "Everything works better that way."

Fleming had been a schoolteacher. Webb had already assigned him the job of keeping books for their operation once they got it set up. Lon was a stickler for precision. His wife had been just the opposite and had run him to distraction with her wild spending and constant demands for more money. Now that she was dead, he wanted to have something for himself and this chance to be part-owner of a big ranch appealed to him.

Webb thought that this had to be a queer partnership. Webb himself had only a part in it. After his parents were murdered, their ranch fell into his hands, but he was forced to run for his life. The murderers controlled the little town of Target, just east of the Webb ranch, and, as long as they were there, Webb could neither run nor sell his ranch.

No one would buy it. The thugs had run off the owners of the two ranches next to Webb's and they couldn't sell their ranches, either.

Then Webb bumped into Bruce Brill, who wanted some land of his own. Webb explained the situation and Brill rounded up the other three old men, and they struck a deal with the owners of the other two ranches. The four old-timers wanted to buy the three ranches, keeping Webb as their foreman, but Clint chose to sell only part of his ranch. That made him a partner of the four men. However, he still accepted the role of foreman.

Now his first task was to take possession of the Webb ranch house. The houses on the other two ranches had been burned. Apparently the men who had taken over intended to keep the Webb house for their own headquarters.

"Got any ideas how to oust that bunch?" Brill asked.

"I'm thinking," Webb said.

"I say let's get them," Gilmore said.

"I agree," Oldham added.

Webb thought that Lon Fleming's name for the four old men was a good one, considering their attitude toward this task. Lon called them the Hawks of Autumn. Certainly they were in the autumn of their lives, and they were real hawks when it came to going after what they wanted.

Not one of the four had any family to worry about them or mourn them if they got killed. None had ever owned anything of real value. This was their last chance and they were more than willing to risk their lives to get the ranch.

"Lon has something," Webb said. "This needs a little planning. But before we can make any definite plans, we need to know the details. I'll slip down there and see what's what."

Bruce Brill fingered the whip looped around his saddle horn. "That don't sound too smart to me," he said. "You're the only one who knows this area and the people. If they kill you, we're all licked."

Brill had worked one season as a bull whacker on a train of freight wagons and learned how to handle a whip. He loved that whip and carried it with him all the time. If he got into a fight, he'd use the whip in preference to a gun if he had a choice.

"I don't plan on getting killed," Webb said. "I just want to see how many men are down there."

"Maybe we ought to bring up Hank and Ike," Fleming said, lifting his hat and rubbing a hand over his bald head.

Webb shook his head. Ike King and Hank

Masters had been left to hold the herd of cattle the hawks had bought to stock their range. They were the only two men the hawks had hired so far.

"We can't leave the cattle unattended," Clint said.

Most of the money the men had pooled for this purchase had gone into that herd of cattle. The land had been cheap because nobody was interested in buying into the trouble that came with it.

Webb moved down the ridge a way so he would have the barn between him and the house. He hoped his companions would stay hidden on the knoll till he got back. Waiting was not one of their greatest virtues. Urging his horse up over the hill, he aimed him directly at the rear of the barn.

Nothing about the ranch had been changed. The Webbs had had a good spread. Clint's father had not been one to give away what was his. When his neighbors had given in to Dude Ronsey and left their ranches, Jim Webb had stayed put—even though his cattle were regularly rustled.

That stubbornness had cost him his life and that of his wife, too. Clint had been gone for a year and, when he returned, he found his parents dead. Of course, Ronsey and his men denied knowing anything about the murders, but Clint didn't believe them.

They allowed him to stay long enough to bury his parents. Then he was told to go. Clint had to run. He couldn't face Ronsey and his henchmen alone. But he had promised himself he would come back and avenge the murder of his parents.

Reining up behind the barn, he counted a dozen horses in the corral. And he had seen two horses tied to the hitchrack in front of the house. He had to find out how many men were here. There might be too many for the hawks to tackle.

Cautiously Clint moved to the corner of the barn to study the house. He knew he couldn't waste much time or the hawks would charge down here to see what was wrong.

He couldn't see any activity around the house, but he had to get close enough to count the men who were here. If there were a dozen or more, as seemed likely, the hawks would have to postpone their strike.

Slipping around the corner of the barn, Clint ran in a crouch to the edge of the house. Moving silently to a window, he peeked inside. He caught his breath. There was a man in there for every horse in the corral, he was sure. He flashed a look over the men. He didn't see a single face that he recognized. These must be Ronsey's men, perhaps the ones who did the rustling.

Clint was still peering cautiously through the window when he felt a sharp jab in his back.

"Don't try nothing foolish!"

Clint froze for an instant, then slowly turned his head. He found himself looking into a face that he did recognize. Tullie Cureton was two or three years younger than Clint. He had always been a sullen boy; now he looked like a dangerous one.

Sid Cureton owned the general store in Target. Tullie and Peggy Cureton were Sid's twins. Webb thought that Peggy was as sweet as a rose, but Tullie was as irritating as the thorns on the bush. He had never understood how twins could be so different.

"Thought you had better sense than to come back here," Tullie said.

"Thought you would have better sense than to try to take over what you don't own," Webb replied.

"I ain't taking it over," Tullie snapped. "But it's a cinch you ain't taking it back."

"Does Ronsey claim it?" Webb asked.

"What if he does?" Tullie said sullenly.

"You don't need that gun in my back," Webb said.

"I ain't sure about that," Tullie said. "Dude has been saying you just might show up again. Come on inside and we'll decide what to do with you."

Clint Webb had no choice. Tullie lifted Webb's gun from its holster and shoved him around the corner of the house toward the door.

As Webb stepped inside, the men suddenly came to attention. Clint saw one other man then that he recognized, Kurt Sikman. He ran the livery barn in Target and was one of Dude Ronsey's main men.

"Just look what you did catch!" Sikman said, a grin splitting his face. "I didn't ever expect to see you again, Clint. Didn't you learn nothing from what happened to your folks?"

Webb didn't answer. He had felt he had a good chance of getting out of this as long as he had only Tullie and some strangers to deal with. But Kurt Sikman put a black cloud in the picture. The real surprise to Webb was that Tullie obviously was a member of Dude Ronsey's outfit.

"What will we do with him?" Tullie asked.

"Well, now," Sikman said, "Dude was talking about the chance that Webb might come back. He don't want him here. So what choice does that leave us?"

"I say we hold him till we can talk to Dude," Tullie said.

"That's why you're a flunky and I'm Dude's right-hand man," Sikman said.

"I ain't no flunky," Tullie shot back. "I'm just as important to Dude as you are."

Sikman snorted. "Like so much hot air, you are. You're just a green pea and you better remember that."

Tullie scowled but said nothing. Webb was surprised that Tullie was so worked up over Sikman's being Dude's main hand. Sikman had held that position for some time, the way Webb remembered it. Sikman had latched on with Ronsey soon after the latter came to town, shortly before Clint had taken off to find his own way in the world.

Clint hoped they would decide to take him to see Dude, since that would give the hawks time to do something about it. If Sikman insisted that he and Tullie had to do something right now, then the hawks wouldn't know anything until it was too late.

"I know Dude wants Webb gone," Sikman said.

"I know that, too," Tullie agreed. "But we'd better let Dude decide what to do."

"I work close with Dude," Sikman said. "I know what he wants."

"You ain't that close to Dude," Tullie shot back.

Sikman's slate-colored eyes seemed to fade. "You pull in your horns, Cureton, or I'll pull them in for you. When Dude ain't here, I'm in charge."

Tullie squared his shoulders and glared at Sikman, but he didn't press the issue. Webb wondered if Tullie would pull his gun on Sikman. He surely wouldn't tackle him in a fist fight. Sikman was over thirty-pounds heavier and had quite a reach on Tullie.

"I'll take care of Webb," Tullie said finally.

"Who said you could?" Sikman demanded. "I'll do it myself."

Webb didn't like the sound of the argument. If they got mad enough at each other, they might both shoot him to prove they could do it.

Under other circumstances, Webb might have taken advantage of the argument to attempt an escape. But with a dozen other men in the room, he wouldn't have much chance.

Sikman jerked out his gun and fired a shot past Webb's head, then laughed when Webb jumped.

"You think that's close? Wait till the next shot."

"If he's got to be shot, I'll do it," Tullie yelled.

"You'll do what I tell you to do," Sikman snapped back. He waved the gun toward Tullie. "You want to argue about this?"

"Dude told me to pull my share of the load," Tullie said sullenly. "I figure on doing it."

"In that case, sit down and shut up. I'm in charge here and you're in my way."

Tullie didn't sit down and he didn't shut up. He stared at Sikman with ill-concealed hatred. "What are you going to do with Webb?"

"Only one thing to do," Sikman said. "Dude sure wants him dead. So I'll take care of it."

He wheeled toward Webb, and Webb knew what he was going to do.

II

There was no time to consider alternatives. Webb threw himself forward as Sikman was whirling toward him. He hit the gunman and they crashed to the floor, the gun exploding, the bullet slamming into the ceiling.

It flashed through Webb's mind that Tullie would likely kill him while he was fighting with Sikman, but he couldn't defend himself against both of them.

Then suddenly another gun roared over the back door. That was followed by a crack like a board splitting, and it seemed to be right above Webb's head.

"On your feet!" a voice roared. "No guns."

Sikman and Webb jerked around to look at the doorway. The hawks were inside the room, guns covering the men. Brill had his whip in his hand. Webb realized it had been the snap of that whip's lash that had popped above his head. Gilmore, Oldham, and Fleming were in a line, each with his gun sweeping the crowd, seeking a defiant one. There were none.

"Either use those guns or shuck them," Oldham said.

Webb could almost see the eagerness in Oldham's eyes. The ex-convict was ready, almost hoping, to start shooting. Apparently the men in the room saw the same thing.

Slowly hands dropped to belt buckles and guns thudded on the floor. Sikman and Tullie were slower to react to the order.

Webb stepped back from Sikman, but the latter had his eyes on the Hawks of Autumn. Right now they looked the part. They were willing to risk more than most men. If anyone could face Ronsey's challenge, these four men could.

Only Tullie Cureton and Kurt Sikman showed any resistance to Oldham's orders. But under the eager threat of his gun, they dropped their belts.

"Looks like we caught the whole litter here," Ace Gilmore said. He looked at Webb. "We've got to get rid of them. Better do it right now."

"We're not murderers," Webb said quickly. He looked over the disarmed men. "If we turn you loose, will you get out of the country?"

Heads nodded eagerly. Webb didn't really believe them. But it was better than a mass murder.

"That's crazy," Oldham said. "You got to take advantage of every break you get. You've caught these skunks in a trap. Don't turn them loose."

Sikman wheeled on his men. "Pick up those guns and fight, you yellowbellies!" he ordered.

Gilmore's gun roared and Sikman's hat flew off his head. "Why don't you pick up your own gun, four-flusher?" he demanded. "Only a coward asks someone else to fight his battles for him."

Sikman turned a light shade of green. He retrieved his hat, staring at the hole in the crown. There was no sign of fight in him now.

"Saddle up your horses and ride fast," Webb said. "This is our ranch. Leave your guns and don't come back."

There was a rush for the door, led by Sikman. Tullie wasn't far behind. Sikman took one of the horses at the hitchrack and Tullie the other. They were well down the road toward town before the other men had caught their horses in the corral and saddled up. The corral was soon empty except for two workhorses that had belonged to Webb's father.

"That was a mistake," Oldham said. "We'll have to deal with them again."

"We couldn't kill them in cold blood," Webb said.

"I've learned that when I let a good opportunity slip away, I usually regret it later," Gilmore said.

"We may regret this, but I won't regret not being a murderer," Clint Webb said.

As the riders left for town, Oldham stepped to the door and fired his gun in the air. Spurs dug in and the horses doubled their speed.

"Funny how a little noise can put the hurry in a bunch of hooligans," Oldham said.

"How'd you happen to be right here when I needed you?" Webb asked.

"We were getting antsy waiting to see what you found down here," Brill said. "Then we heard a shot and came down as hard as we could ride. Figured you might need a little help."

"I needed more than a little," Webb said. He looked around. "We've got this house to ourselves after we get it cleaned up. What we need now is supplies."

"How far to a town where we can buy something?" Brill asked.

"Three miles to Target," Webb said. "Sid Cureton runs the general store there unless there's been a change since I left. I think he'll still sell to us."

"What about those rannies we fired out of here?"

"They could cause trouble," Webb admitted. "But not now. They got to lay hold of some guns. Anyway, we have to get supplies. If we're going to live here and run this ranch, we can't be afraid to go to town."

Gilmore grunted. "Who's afraid? If I was your age, I'd be scared. But those days are gone for me. Let's go get what we need."

They decided it was best to keep together, so they had to leave the house unguarded. Webb got his horse from behind the barn while the others mounted up.

"The men we ran out of here may just keep on going," Webb said. "They probably didn't bargain for a fight when they hired on."

"Who do you think hired them?" Brill asked.

"Dude Ronsey," Webb said. "I think they rustle cattle for him. We lost almost all the cattle we had before someone killed my parents."

"We ought to find out for sure who killed your folks and return the favor," Oldham said.

"That's my job," Webb said grimly, "and I intend to do it."

They rode cautiously on their way to town. There was no good place in the flat countryside for an ambush, but they were taking no chances.

The only street in the town ran north and south. They hit that road south of town and rode slowly up it. On the left side was the general store Webb remembered. The Curetons lived above the store. On the right was the hardware store. Norm Pinburg ran that and the Pinburgs had a house just a short distance behind the store.

Further up the street, was the town's saloon. Dude Ronsey owned that and had his bachelor living quarters in a couple of rooms added to the back. Across the street was Kurt Sikman's livery barn. Sikman lived in a shack fifty yards behind the barn. There was little else in Target, Nebraska. Broken Horn Creek ran just behind the saloon and hardware store on its way to the Platte.

Reining up in front of the general store, Webb

dismounted and led his men inside. Fleming stayed close to the door where he could watch the horses and the street.

Sid Cureton was obviously surprised to see Clint Webb. Webb knew then that the men they had run off the ranch hadn't been in the store.

"We need a lot of things, Sid," Webb said.

"Always glad to get an order," Cureton said. "Don't do much business here since so many of the ranchers pulled out."

"We're staying," Webb said. He handed the storekeeper a list of what they needed.

Cureton hurried off to fill the order. He was nervous, obviously frightened by Webb's return. Cureton was not one to enjoy conflict, yet in Ronsey's town, he must live on the edge of it constantly.

Peggy Cureton came down the stairs from the living quarters overhead. Webb thought she hadn't changed since he'd last seen her. It hadn't really been that long, but it seemed ages ago that he'd come into town once or twice a week to buy something for the ranch, always volunteering for the job so he could see Peggy.

She was a foot shorter than Webb and at least seventy pounds lighter. He'd told her once she weighed about as much as his shadow. Her hazel eyes had always haunted him. It seemed to Webb that she was prettier than he remembered, but maybe it was because he hadn't seen her for a while.

The surprise on her face was proof that his appearance was totally unexpected.

"When did you get back?" she asked. "And—and why?"

"It's my land," Webb said. "I sold part of it to my partners here. But nobody else has any claim on it."

"I'm glad you're back," she said. "But, Clint, Dude Ronsey says the Webb ranch is his now."

"That's a lie," Webb said. "After my parents were killed, I inherited it. I sold part of it to these men. They also bought out Carson and Mullen. I'm foreman of the whole outfit. Ronsey's men won't be there anymore."

"I smell trouble," Sid Cureton said.

"I do, too," Webb said. "But my partners and I are there to stay."

"We had planned a dance at your place a week after the Fourth of July," Peggy said. "There's no place in town big enough. Suppose we can still have it there?"

Webb shrugged. "I see no reason why not unless you can't get anybody from town to go out there."

"We can get them there," Peggy said positively. "Elizabeth Pinburg and I are planning it. Maybe the dance will help calm things down."

"Or maybe blow things sky high," Sid Cureton said.

"I play a good fiddle," Lon Fleming put in. "Need a player?"

"We surely do," Peggy said excitedly. She turned to Webb. "Will you go over with me to Elizabeth's? We'll tell her what's happened."

Webb wasn't sure why he was needed, but he was willing to go, just to be with Peggy. The hawks disapproved, but they promised to alert him if anybody came down from the saloon.

As bookkeeper for the ranch, Fleming was put in charge of getting the supplies they needed while Webb was gone. Webb and Peggy moved cautiously across the street and to the Pinburg house behind the hardware store.

Elizabeth Pinburg was as excited about the dance as Peggy. Webb knew there was almost no social life in Target. This dance must be the highlight of the year for them.

Elizabeth was a sharp contrast to Peggy. She was five inches taller and about thirty pounds heavier with black hair and brown eyes. Not as pretty as Peggy, in Webb's eyes, but a nice-looking girl.

The girls talked a little about the Fourth of July celebration planned for town, but mostly they talked about the dance to be held a week later.

Webb and Peggy got back to the general store without incident and Webb found Oldham and

Gilmore wanting to go to the saloon. Webb squelched that idea. Most likely Ronsey's men would be there, and by now they would probably be armed again.

"We've got to face them sometime," Oldham said.

"Not on their own ground," Webb said. He turned to Sid Cureton. "Have you heard anything that would help me prove who killed my folks?"

Cureton backed off nervously. "I don't hear much anymore. Hardly anybody comes in here except for grub and they buy that in a hurry and get out."

Webb guessed that might be true. He didn't know exactly what connection Cureton had with Ronsey, but he knew it was something. There wasn't a man in Target who didn't bow and scrape to Dude Ronsey. Ronsey owned the town and now he wanted to own all the ranches near it.

Peggy motioned Webb off to the back of the store. He followed, wondering what she had in mind.

"I have three goats," she said. "Two are nannies. Pa has a nervous stomach and has to have goat's milk, the doctor says. My problem is the billy goat. He gets out of his pen and makes life miserable for everybody. Dude Ronsey says I have to get rid of him. Would it be possible to put him out at your ranch? There is that tight calf pen that should hold him."

Webb wasn't too keen about caring for a goat, but it was Peggy asking. He agreed to let her bring him out there.

"I'll be out now and then and help take care of him," Peggy said. "I'll pay you for keeping him."

"Does Ronsey boss everything you do?" Webb asked.

She sighed. "Almost. Pa is in no shape to argue with him. He gets an upset stomach every time Dude comes around."

"Does Dude treat Norm Pinburg that way, too?"

"I think so, but Mr. Pinburg doesn't have a nervous stomach like Pa does."

"Why do you stay here?"

"We're making a good living here. Pa just never could make it anywhere else."

That didn't answer Webb's question, but he knew it was as close as Peggy was going to get. He wondered how they could make a good living when Sid had said that hardly anybody came in the store. Webb thought of Tullie. He wanted to ask Peggy about her twin brother, but he didn't. Tullie must be on the payroll of Ronsey, but Webb wasn't going to mention that to Peggy.

Fleming gathered up their supplies and each man took some in his saddlebags. Then they headed back to the ranch.

Bruce Brill brought up the question Webb was sure they were all thinking. "Just what is the setup here? Looks like Ronsey owns the town, yet you're friendly with the storekeeper, especially his daughter."

"Ronsey has some hold on Sid Cureton. I don't know what," Webb said. "He has a reason for everything he does and everything has to bring him a profit. I thought he might strike back at us when we were in town. But just because he didn't doesn't mean he won't when he can pick the time and place."

"Maybe his men don't have new guns yet," Fleming said.

"Maybe," Webb agreed. "We did take all their guns from them. But they won't be without weapons for long."

"Looks to me like we'll have to clean out that town before we can make any money ranching," Brill said.

"Not the whole town," Webb said. "I don't think Sid Cureton or Norm Pinburg will do us any damage. But I don't trust Sikman or Ronsey or any of his men."

"We should of shown them who was boss when we had them disarmed," Gilmore said. "When you get an advantage, you have to make something out of it."

Webb knew he wasn't going to hear the last of that. These men were truly hawks. Once they struck a prey, they followed through for the kill.

By late afternoon the men had cleaned up the house and put away their supplies. Their cattle were being held several miles to the west and they were thinking about riding out to check on them when Fleming passed a window and announced, “Company coming.”

Webb rushed over. There shouldn’t be any company unless Peggy was bringing out the goat. One look and Webb knew it wasn’t Peggy. Three riders were moving leisurely toward the ranch.

“Know them?” Gilmore asked.

Webb nodded. “The one in the middle is Dude Ronsey. On his right is his bartender, Quince Tucker. He’s always with Ronsey, like a body-guard. You’ve met the man on his left. That’s Kurt Sikman. You put a bullet through his hat this morning, Ace.”

Webb wondered if this was the showdown he knew would have to come before peace could settle over the valley.

Clint Webb searched the flats on either side of the road, but he didn’t see the small army that Ronsey had at his command. Yet that didn’t ease the flutter in his stomach.

III

Webb stayed at the window as the men rode closer. He had to make a decision quickly, before those three got to the hitchrack in front. If they were coming in peace, he'd react in the same vein. But if they were coming to throw him and his partners off the ranch, he had to be prepared.

"If that's the head honcho, we'd better get rid of him," Oldham said at Webb's elbow.

"We don't know that he's coming for war," Webb said.

"You said we'd have to fight to stay here," Gilmore said. "This looks like a good place to start."

Fleming and Brill were at another window watching the approach of Ronsey and his two men.

"They don't look like they're coming for war," Fleming said.

Webb had to agree. He couldn't imagine anyone riding in as openly and leisurely as these men were doing if they were looking for immediate trouble. Webb searched the horizon again for a trap. It appeared that Ronsey was coming with only his two right-hand men. He didn't know what to make of it.

"If we put these three out of commission, we have the whole outfit licked, don't we?" Oldham said.

"We'd have our necks in a noose for murder," Webb said, "unless we could prove they were here to murder us."

"That wouldn't be easy to do unless they started the shooting," Fleming said.

And they had no proof that Ronsey had done anything wrong. Webb made a decision. The men were only a hundred yards away. He couldn't stall any longer.

"Ace, you and Jay come with me." Gilmore and Oldham stepped toward the door eagerly.

"Bruce, you and Lon cover us from the windows," Webb added. "Absolutely no shooting unless they start it."

Webb knew he couldn't trust either Oldham or Gilmore not to start a shootout if he left them back in the house. But he was sure that Fleming wouldn't start anything. He was always looking for a peaceful solution to every problem. And Brill was the most level-headed one of the four. He wouldn't shoot until shot at.

As the trio rode up and stopped at the hitchrack, Webb opened the door and moved outside. Gilmore and Oldham were just a step behind him.

The three riders stayed in their saddles as Clint Webb moved down to the hitchrack.

"Are you here in peace?" Clint asked.

"Absolutely," Ronsey said, his voice gentle. "We didn't think it necessary to carry a flag of truce."

"Just wanted to be sure," Webb said. "Get down."

The three dismounted. Ronsey must have known that five men had run his men off the ranch. Only three stood before him now. Ronsey's eyes flashed across the front of the house, apparently looking for the other two.

"I came to apologize for my men being in your house when you came," Ronsey said. "We thought the house was deserted, so we were letting them use it."

Webb thought back to the day Ronsey had tried to buy the ranch from his father for about five percent of its worth. If he hadn't known better, he wouldn't have thought this seemingly peaceable person was the same man.

"I found some partners," Webb said. "We don't want any trouble—just a chance to run the ranch without interference."

"You'll get it," Ronsey said, smiling. "I came out to set things straight."

Webb couldn't believe that. But if Ronsey wanted to play games, he'd go along with it for now.

"Also," Ronsey went on, "we came out to invite you to our little Fourth of July celebration. Target isn't big enough for much of a bash, but we'll have a good horse race and some fireworks."

"Horse race?" Gilmore said, his black eyes lighting up.

"You like a race?" Ronsey said, glancing at Gilmore.

"Always did," the ex-gambler said. "I've won and lost a lot of money on horse races."

"Wouldn't happen to have a horse you'd like to run in the race, would you?" Sikman put in.

"I might," Gilmore said.

"Bring him in on the Fourth and run him," Ronsey invited.

"How about a small bet?" Sikman asked.

Gilmore's eyes flashed. "Sure thing. How much?"

"I'm betting on Mr. Ronsey's horse," Sikman said. "Ten dollars."

"I'll cover that," Gilmore said.

"I'll put twenty on my horse, too," Ronsey said.

Gilmore covered that bet and another twenty-dollar bet by Tucker, the bartender. Before Webb could say anything, Gilmore had put up fifty dollars. That was a lot of money and Ronsey must have a sure thing or he and his men wouldn't bet so freely. Of course, Gilmore had a good horse, too. They were keeping it with the cattle herd, out of trouble. He had won some races with that horse.

Webb saw the men looking at the horses in the corral. They were good cow ponies but not racers. Most likely Ronsey and his friends thought they'd be running against one of them.

Let them think so. They'd be in for more of a race than they counted on.

Ronsey swung back into the saddle. Sikman and Tucker did the same. "We'll see you at the celebration," Ronsey called as they reined around toward town.

"What do you make of that?" Gilmore asked when they were gone.

"You just risked fifty dollars we can't afford to lose," Webb said.

"I ain't lost it yet," Gilmore protested. "Ain't many horses can beat Blue Boy."

"Likely Ronsey has one that can," Webb said. "I've heard that his horse has never lost a race."

Fleming and Brill came from the house to watch the three riders disappear.

"Looks like all our worries were for nothing," Fleming said.

"I wouldn't bet on that, either," Webb said. "Ronsey wants to feel us out. He wanted this ranch before Pa and Ma were killed. Then he had it till we got here. You can bet he plans to get it back."

"We should have torn them apart while they were here," Oldham said. "We could have taken them, especially with two guns in the house helping us."

"The longer we can put off the showdown, if it comes to that, the better chance we'll have," Webb said. "Maybe we can scare off some of his men."

"Who is going to ride your horse for you?" Brill asked Gilmore.

"I usually ride him myself," the gambler said.

"You weigh over two hundred pounds," Webb exclaimed. "An old mule could beat you. You need a small jockey. You can bet Ronsey will have one."

Gilmore frowned. "I hadn't thought of that. I just know how fast Blue Boy can run."

"Not carrying two hundred pounds," Fleming said. "None of us are jockeys. You need someone about a hundred pounds."

"Ain't no kids around here," Gilmore said.

The Fourth was only a few days away, so there would be little time to get ready for the race. Gilmore might have to ride his own horse. If so, Webb was sure the hawk would lose his fifty dollars.

An hour later, a wagon came toward the ranch. Again Webb was on the alert, but he didn't expect any danger from a wagon.

When the wagon got close enough, he could see a man and a woman in it, and they were hauling something in the wagon bed behind them. Then he recognized Sid Cureton and Peggy. Their cargo was a big crate.

"We've got a goat coming," Webb announced. "Let's check the fence on that calf pen."

"Ain't no pen made that can keep a goat in if he wants out," Brill grumbled.

"I take it you don't like goats," Webb said.

"Goats and sheep!" Brill said disgustedly. "Ain't no difference except some goats have horns."

"There is a distinct difference," Fleming corrected. "Goats are more independent. They climb on things. They butt anything that gets in their way. Sheep follow a leader and are virtually helpless."

Webb grinned. The schoolteacher popped out in Fleming at the slightest provocation. He watched the wagon pull into the yard.

"We had some trouble getting Dynamite into that crate," Sid Cureton announced. "It wasn't his idea of the way to travel."

"I hope he won't be a nuisance to you," Peggy said. "Dude Ronsey said we had to get him out of town."

"What's Ronsey got against a goat?" Webb asked.

"Everybody teases Dynamite," she said. "Quince Tucker and Dude Ronsey are the worst. Dynamite doesn't forget who's tormented him. Every time he gets out of his pen, he goes looking for those men. If he finds them, they have to do some fancy stepping to get out of his way."

Webb grinned. "I'd like to see that."

Peggy laughed. "It's quite a sight. But it's something Mr. Ronsey won't put up with. So we have to keep Dynamite out of trouble."

"Young goats are good eating," Sid put in.

"And Doc says I've got to have goat's milk for my nervous stomach. So we need to raise goats. We'll keep the nannies in town where we can milk them. They don't bother anyone much. It's just Dynamite that raises cain."

"I hope he doesn't do the same here," Oldham said, eyeing the goat suspiciously.

Webb checked the fence on the calf pen. It was sheep fencing and fairly high. It had always kept in the calves that the Webbs had had to feed by hand when a cow died or wouldn't claim her calf. He hoped it would hold a goat. But he wasn't sure.

"Does Ronsey really run the town?" Gilmore asked as he helped lift the crate out of the wagon.

"Just about," Cureton admitted. "Nobody can buck him and come out ahead."

"Ronsey was out here this afternoon," Webb said. "Was nice as apple pie. What's he up to?"

Cureton shook his head. "I've no idea. He isn't overly nice most of the time."

"Hardly any of the time," Peggy put in.

Webb turned his attention to Peggy. "Do you think he's up to something?"

"He always is," Peggy said.

"Hush, Peggy," her father said. "You don't know that."

"It seems like it, anyway," Peggy said, looking away from her father.

Webb knew that she had meant what she said.

Ronsey impressed Webb as a man who had a single purpose in life—to gain everything he wanted with no regard as to who might suffer in the process. If he wasn't up to something now, he'd be up to something later. Maybe after the celebration.

They got the crate to the gate of the calf pen and Cureton lifted the door in the crate. The goat had to move backward, but he felt the door behind him disappear and he backed out quickly. The men pulled the crate away and shut the calf-pen gate. The goat stared around at the confining fence and walked slowly back and forth, examining his new quarters.

When Dynamite had quieted down and it seemed he would stay in the pen, Sid Cureton and Peggy drove back to town, leaving the crate near the pen.

"Heard you talking about Ronsey," Brill said. "What did Cureton think about him?"

"He's not in a position to say what he thinks," Webb said. "But Peggy says what she thinks and she thinks he's up to something."

"We ain't likely to have any real peace until we clean out that town," Brill predicted.

"Maybe," Webb said.

He suddenly thought of the locket his mother had always worn. She had told him once that if anything happened to her, he was to open the locket and he'd find something she didn't want him to know until after she was dead.

When he had found his parents dead, he had looked for the locket, but it was gone. Obviously the killer had taken it. Now Clint wanted to find the locket for another reason. When he found it, he'd surely find the killer.

"I figure rustlers might try to take our herd," Webb said. "I'm convinced Ronsey was behind the rustling when we lived here. I'm going to ride out and stay with the herd tonight."

At dusk Gilmore went along with Webb. He wanted to get Blue Boy ready for the race on the Fourth.

They found the herd roughly where they had left it. Ike King said nothing had happened since the others had left. Hank Masters was close by with the extra horses. Webb went with Gilmore and caught the blue roan. He was a poor-looking horse for a racer, but Webb knew his looks belied his speed. He wished he knew what kind of horse Ronsey had.

The night went by uneventfully. Maybe Ronsey didn't know yet that the hawks had a herd of cattle on the ranch. Before Webb and Gilmore left the next morning, Webb gave the two men instructions to bring the herd closer to the ranch house.

Even though nothing had happened, Webb knew Brill was right. They'd have no peace as long as Ronsey and his men were within striking distance.

They found the ranch house in a turmoil. The billy goat had gotten out of his pen during the night and had come into the house to make himself at home. The three occupants had objected, especially Oldham. They had spent two hours corralling the goat and putting him back in the pen. Then they had spent another hour raising the fence so he couldn't jump over it again. Oldham was ready to kill the goat.

Luckily Oldham had quieted down by the time breakfast was over. Checking out the window, Webb saw a rider off to the north. He went outside and took a look. Twice he saw riders off to the north toward the sandhills; once down toward the river. He was sure those were Ronsey's men and he was willing to bet they weren't planning anything good for him and his four partners.

The sun was a couple of hours high when a rider appeared on the road from town. It took Webb only a few seconds to identify the rider as Peggy. Probably coming out to see how her goat was doing. Webb warned the men not to say too much about the goat getting out.

Peggy wasn't surprised about the escape. She helped the men strengthen the fence to make sure Dynamite didn't get out again.

Webb called Peggy's attention to a couple of riders off to the north. "I've seen them three or four times this morning. What do you think Ronsey is up to?"

"Are you sure they're Ronsey's men?" she asked.

"Who else would be riding around in this area?" he asked.

"You have a point there," she said. "I've never been able to figure out what Dude Ronsey will do next. But it is never anything for the good of anybody but Dude Ronsey."

Webb nodded. "I'll bet on that."

IV

As Peggy rode back to town, she watched the riders to the north and south. They had to be Dude Ronsey's men. There wasn't anyone else around.

What was Dude up to? She knew Ronsey too well to believe he'd give up the ranch without a fight. He wanted that ranch. After the Webbs were killed, Dude had taken over the ranch just as if he'd bought and paid for it.

Peggy wondered how Clint and those four old men had ousted Ronsey's crew. She wished she could have seen that. Five men against twelve and the twelve had run. Dude Ronsey would strike back.

Whatever he did, Peggy hoped it wouldn't involve her father. Sid Cureton was not a fighter, yet he had to do whatever Ronsey told him.

She tried to put that out of her mind. She got angry every time she allowed herself to think of it. Peggy turned her thoughts to more pleasant things, like the upcoming Fourth of July celebration.

Now that Ronsey had run out all the neighboring ranchers, there really wasn't anyone to come to the celebration but Ronsey's men and maybe a few cowboys from several miles down the valley. For the men the highlight of the celebration had always been the horse race, but there wasn't much suspense to it anymore. Even last year, when some of the ranchers were still here, the race had been closed to anyone who didn't work for Ronsey. None of his men had horses that could best Ronsey's, and Ronsey could only bet with someone foolish enough to give away his money.

Peggy thought of Gilmore and his challenge of Dude's horse. Likely Gilmore didn't have a chance, either. He simply wouldn't expect Ronsey to have a real racer. Nobody expected that out here. Webb might know better, but he didn't control the four old men. Peggy grinned to herself. She doubted if anybody controlled them. They were like a breath of fresh air in a stale room.

Ronsey would have Fad Vernon ride his horse. He always did, whenever he could drum up a race with anyone. Fad was a very small man, just about Peggy's size, and she was smaller than most women. Fad was not too bright. He was about twenty-one years old, but he had the brains of a seven-year-old.

He got real enjoyment out of riding Ronsey's racer, but he was kicked around the rest of the time by Ronsey and his men, doing all the dirty work that they didn't want to do.

Peggy felt sorry for Fad, but right now her mind

toyed with the dream that somehow Gilmore's horse could beat Ronsey's racer. She should have asked to see the horse they were going to race. Meanwhile, in town, there was only one question to be discussed—by how much would Ronsey's horse beat the challenger?

Peggy wondered who would ride Gilmore's horse. Certainly none of the four old men were spry enough or small enough to make a good jockey. Webb might be young enough, but he was not a small man, standing over six feet tall, and Peggy guessed he would weigh at least a hundred and eighty pounds. That weight alone would be too much for the horse even if he was a racer.

If Gilmore's horse had even an outside chance of staying in the race with Ronsey's horse, she might volunteer to ride. Given a mount as good as the one Fad would ride, she felt sure she could win. She was a better rider than Fad.

Peggy could imagine the look on Dude Ronsey's face if he heard that she was riding Gilmore's horse in the race. She wouldn't let him know until the last minute if she should decide to do it.

Then she realized that she was dreaming. The old men probably wouldn't let her ride. Anyway, it would be a miracle if Gilmore's horse had a chance against Ronsey's racer. She didn't want to get involved unless she had a chance to win.

The minute Peggy stepped into the store, she forgot about the race. Sid Cureton was sitting on a stool behind the counter and he had that depressed stare that she had come to recognize. She didn't say anything to him but turned to her mother. Winona Cureton was the strength in the family.

"What happened to Pa?" Peggy asked softly.

"He's just come from a meeting that Dude called," Winona said, a frown furrowing her forehead. "He won't say much, but apparently something's afoot that he doesn't like."

"Does it have something to do with the men on the Webb ranch?"

Winona shrugged, but frowned harder. "He won't say. But what else can it be? Dude had everything going his way till these men came. I can't imagine how four old men and Clint can scare him."

"There's something about those men, Ma. They're not ordinary men. And Clint isn't the same, either. If Dude tries to run them off the ranch, he may find it tougher than he thinks."

Winona sighed disgustedly.

"Your father won't say what Dude talked about, but it's upset him. His stomach will act up again, that's sure."

"Why does Dude want that ranch, anyway?" Peggy asked. "He doesn't run any cattle there."

"Maybe he plans to stock it," said her mother.

"Anyway, he seems very upset because those old men are out there."

Peggy again thought of the race. If Gilmore's horse should win that, it would rub salt in the wound for Ronsey. She wanted to know what Ronsey had talked about at the meeting. Maybe Elizabeth Pinburg would know.

Elizabeth was the only girl near Peggy's age in Target, and they gravitated to each other through necessity. Peggy headed across the street, past the hardware store to the Pinburg house.

However, Elizabeth had run into the same blank wall that Peggy had. Norm Pinburg wouldn't say what the meeting had been about.

"I think your pa is in the same boat as mine," Elizabeth said. "They have to kowtow to Dude, but they don't get into any trouble if they do. I think we ought to be glad they've got good stores and Dude's men buy enough to keep them going."

Peggy wasn't sure that was good reasoning. She had often wondered how they could live as well as they did on the profit from the few groceries they sold in the store. Dude Ronsey had something to do with that and Peggy had the feeling it was Sid's bowing to Ronsey's bidding that netted him a good living for his family.

"You think we should keep quiet and not tip the wagon?" Peggy asked.

Elizabeth nodded. "I don't know just what is

going on, but we've got a decent living. Pa was never able to make ends meet before we came here."

Peggy understood that. She could remember when Dude Ronsey first came into their lives. That had been back in Omaha. Dude showed up in their store when Sid Cureton was barely scratching out an existence. Then suddenly they were doing quite well and Ronsey hinted clearly that he was responsible.

Ronsey left town then and it wasn't long until Sid got a letter inviting him to come to take over a general store that Ronsey had bought. Sid hadn't hesitated and the family had landed in Target. It was a tiny town when the Curetons arrived.

Then Sikman came and started a livery barn, and Norm Pinburg arrived to build a hardware store. Ronsey built a saloon, and that was the extent of the present town. Twice, other people had come to begin businesses, but they soon left. This was Ronsey's town and all the people in it were his. Peggy had never figured out why he wanted it that way, but there was no doubt about its being a fact.

Peggy left, hoping to find someone who would tell her what that meeting was about. The town, only a block long, was divided into two sections. The general store and the hardware were at the south end of town while the saloon and the livery stable were at the north end.

The corral ran out south of the livery barn, over halfway down to the general store. Kurt Sikman was down at the south end of the corral when Peggy came back across the street from Pinburg's.

Peggy wasn't fond of Kurt Sikman, but she knew he was close to Dude Ronsey. He was sure to know what that meeting had been about. She angled over to the corral fence.

"Say, Kurt, were you at the meeting up at the saloon?" she asked.

"Sure," Sikman said. He gave her a big grin. Peggy shrank back from him. She and Elizabeth Pinburg were the only single girls in town and Sikman was a bachelor. Neither she nor Elizabeth thought much of Kurt. Peggy was almost afraid of him.

"What was the meeting about?" she asked.

"Ask your pa," Sikman said. "He was there." He grinned again. "But I can tell you those newcomers are in for a surprise."

Peggy tried another question or two, but Sikman wouldn't say any more about the meeting. At least, she knew that it concerned Webb and the four old men.

She saw Quince Tucker, the bartender, standing in front of the saloon. Quince was younger than Sikman and also a bachelor. Peggy was deathly afraid of him. He was Ronsey's bodyguard and a killer, she was sure.

Peggy turned quickly back to the store. Her twin brother, Tullie, was inside when she got there. Maybe he had been at the meeting. She worried about him. He seemed to be growing away from the family. He spent too much time in Ronsey's saloon.

"I suppose you were at Dude's meeting this morning," she said.

"Sure thing," Tullie replied proudly. "He depends on me being there when anything important comes up."

"What was so important about today's meeting?" Peggy asked.

"None of your business," Tullie snapped. Lately he turned surly at the slightest provocation.

"I just don't want you doing something you'll regret someday," she said.

"The only regret I'll have is if I don't get a shot at those newcomers," he snapped back.

Tullie went up the stairs to the Curetons' living quarters. Peggy let him go. He was taking great pride in his standing with Dude Ronsey. That worried her more than the meeting itself.

But Peggy now knew that Ronsey was aiming some kind of trouble at Webb and the old men, and this worried her, too. She liked Clint Webb. She'd liked him before he left town; she liked him even more now. He had said he needed to be out on his own or he'd never learn to cope in a wild country like this—and he was right. He'd come back a much stronger, more determined man. She also liked those four old men. She'd heard Webb call them the hawks. They did remind her of sharp-eyed birds of prey.

She wished the Curetons could get out from under Dude Ronsey's domination. But there wasn't much chance of that happening. No one could beat Dude Ronsey. She was still puzzled as to how Webb and the hawks had driven Ronsey's men off the ranch.

Tullie had said something that made her suspect that he had been there, too. And that was upsetting.

Peggy tried talking to her father, but he was still in a deep depression and wouldn't respond to her questions. They must have planned something awful at the saloon meeting. She turned to her mother. Winona had a sharp sense of what was going on and she was always willing to express her opinion.

"What do you think Dude is up to, Ma?" Peggy asked when she got her mother off at the far end of the store.

"He's set on running out the newcomers," Winona said. "Pa doesn't like violence and Dude lives by it. I'm afraid Tullie is getting in deeper with Dude all the time."

"I think he was at the ranch when Webb and the old men ran them off," Peggy said.

"I'm sure he was. And now I think he feels he has to redeem himself in Dude's eyes."

That made sense to Peggy, and she didn't like what it was doing to her twin brother. She thought of the race coming up.

"What about Fad Vernon?" she asked. "Where does he fit in?"

"I've been trying to find out. Gertie Pinburg says he's an orphan that Dude picked up to do the hard work that he considers his men too good to do. From the way Fad works, that may be the truth."

"Do you think Dude's men killed Clint's parents?" Peggy asked in a whisper.

"Your guess is as good as mine," Winona said. "But who else is there around here who could have done it?"

That answered Peggy's question. "Do you think they're afraid of Clint?"

Winona nodded. "Could be. Clint Webb may be out to get the murderers of his parents. I hope he does find them and evens the score."

Peggy looked sharply at her mother, who didn't usually put such emphasis on her words. "I wish we were out of Target," she said.

"I wish we'd never come," Winona said. "Sid keeps saying we have a good living here. But Dude has us under his thumb and someday he's going to squash us."

Those were depressing words to Peggy. She

couldn't deny the truth in them, though. She went outside. Getting on her horse, she headed back out to the ranch. She wanted a look at Gilmore's racehorse. If she could ride him to victory, she'd get some real satisfaction out of it. Even the tiniest thing that would strike back at Ronsey would be a victory for her.

At the ranch, Webb and two of the old men came out to meet her. The other two were out with their cattle, Webb said.

"I want to see the horse you're racing against Dude tomorrow," Peggy said.

Gilmore was curious. "Want to tell Ronsey about him?"

Peggy said, "I want to ride him if he's a good one. I want to beat Dude. He'll have little Fad Vernon riding his horse."

They went down to the corral and Gilmore led the way inside the barn. He opened a door to a box stall. A blue roan horse came up and nuzzled Gilmore. He was scrubby looking but long-legged.

"Can I ride him to see what he's like?" Peggy asked.

"Sure," Gilmore said. "We don't have a rider for the race. I was a fool to bet Ronsey, I reckon, but I can't stand his arrogance."

Gilmore saddled the blue roan and led him out of the barn. "Want me to top him off? He's a little foxy."

"I can handle him," Peggy said confidently. "What's his name?"

"Blue Boy," Gilmore said proudly. "He can run."

Peggy swung up into the saddle and petted the horse's neck. The horse didn't even bow his back. He was ready to run. Peggy let him have some rein and he swept across the flat bottomland, then circled back toward the barn. Now that he was warmed up, she loosened the reins. She knew she was on a racer then. He seemed to flatten to the ground and shot over the grass like a frightened rabbit.

"Will you let me ride him in the race?" Peggy asked eagerly when she had brought the horse to a halt at the barn.

"You bet," Gilmore said. "And I'll lay more money on Blue Boy before the race, too."

"What will Ronsey say to this?" Webb asked.

"I hope it makes him mad," Peggy said. "This is the chance I've been waiting for. He always gets his way. Maybe this time he won't. Don't let Dude see Blue Boy before the race."

Gilmore promised and Peggy hurried back to town. Before she dismounted, she saw Tullie and Sikman arguing at the side of the general store. She didn't want to get involved, but she was always afraid that Tullie would get in a fight. He had the meanness for a fight but not the wits. Fortunately Sikman broke off the argument and headed for the livery barn.

"What was that about?" Peggy demanded when Tullie came back to the front of the store.

"He thinks he's going to keep on being Dude's right-hand man," Tullie snapped. "Well, I'm his right-hand man now, even if Kurt doesn't know it."

"You don't want to be Dude's man," Peggy said.

Tullie, still driven by anger from his argument, turned on his sister. "Look, I'm getting up in the world and I'm going to go higher. Quince Tucker is Dude's bodyguard and Kurt was once his right-hand man. I'm taking Kurt's place now and I may take Quince's place before long."

"Why do you want to be so close to Dude?" Peggy asked, fear creeping into her voice.

"Dude is the biggest thing in the Platte Valley and I aim to be a part of it. We're going to get rid of that bunch of scum who've moved in on the ranch. I'll take care of Clint Webb personally."

"I don't want you involved in fighting those men," Peggy insisted.

"Who cares what you want?" Tullie snapped and stalked into the store.

Peggy got back on her horse. The mood Tullie was in might result in almost anything. Especially on top of that saloon meeting. Even if he was her twin brother, she had to warn the hawks.

At the ranch, she met Webb and the two men

who'd been there before. Worry was plain in Webb's face.

"What's wrong, Peggy?" he demanded. "You just left here a half hour ago."

"Dude had a meeting to get rid of you and your friends," Peggy said. "Tullie has threatened to kill you himself." Tears were just behind her words.

V

Webb stared at Peggy. He felt the jolt even though he had known that Ronsey would try something before long. But he had felt sure he'd wait until after the celebration.

"Does this mean that you won't ride Blue Boy in the race?" Gilmore asked slowly.

Peggy shook her head. "I want to ride him and I want to beat Dude's horse more than anything I can think of. But if you come to the celebration, don't trust any of Dude's men."

"We won't let our guard down," Webb promised.

"I'll be back tomorrow to work out Blue Boy and get him used to me," Peggy said, the worry still etched in her face.

"Won't Ronsey give you trouble if you ride our horse?" Webb asked.

Peggy shook her head. "Dude knows I'm a rebel, but he never gives me any trouble. I'd do it, anyway, 'cause I know I have a chance of beating him."

She reined her horse around toward town. Webb watched her go. She had made this trip out here just to warn them. Ace Gilmore had been arguing that there was real trouble brewing, but Lon Fleming hadn't agreed. Of the four hawks,

Fleming was the one who might be called a misfit. He would look for a peaceful solution to any problem that arose, though he would fight if there was no alternative. The other three couldn't even think of a solution other than force.

Thinking of Peggy's warning, Webb was surprised that Ronsey would let it be known what he had in mind. Or maybe he hadn't intended Peggy to find out.

It would be hard on Peggy if anything happened to her twin brother, Tullie. But she had warned Webb to watch for Tullie in particular. Webb remembered Tullie as a very impulsive young fellow even before he left the ranch. He had not been an easy one to get along with then and Webb guessed that he would make a very formidable foe now.

"Why did she have to come out here with that story," Fleming asked after Peggy was gone. "Things were going so well."

"That's why she came," Webb said. "We've been acting like we thought there wasn't going to be any trouble. She knows there is and she wants to make sure we know it, too. We owe her our thanks."

"Maybe I ought to ride out and bring in Oldham and Brill," Gilmore said.

"We can handle things here," Webb said. "Anyway, Ronsey's men might strike at the herd. They stole practically all our cattle before they killed my parents. They might follow the same pattern now."

Gilmore nodded and turned to look down the road toward town. Fleming shook his head and went inside. He apparently wasn't convinced that Ronsey meant anything more warlike than a horse race between them.

Late in the afternoon, Gilmore, who was still watching the road, pointed to a couple of distant dots. "Looks like somebody's coming," he said.

Webb agreed. There wasn't much chance that anyone on that road was headed anywhere but to the ranch.

"I'm going to make sure Blue Boy is out of sight in that box stall," Gilmore said.

Clint nodded. Gilmore knew the betting advantage of springing a good horse on the unsuspecting opposition.

Fleming came out of the house when he saw the riders coming. For several minutes they watched the riders come closer. They seemed to be in no hurry. Finally they got close enough for Webb to recognize Dude Ronsey and Quince Tucker. Ronsey never seemed to go anywhere without Tucker.

"I told you they weren't gunning for us," Fleming said. "That's not the way they'd come if they meant trouble."

"Probably not," Webb said. "But it will pay us to keep our guard up, anyway."

"They're coming to look at my horse," Gilmore said in a lower tone as the riders turned into the yard.

Webb watched them closely. He believed what Peggy had told him. In fact, he'd never believed anything but the worst about Dude Ronsey. The saloon owner's eyes raced over the house and yard and outbuildings.

"We were just checking to make sure you intended to show up tomorrow," Ronsey said. "I have some people who want to make bets on the race and I don't like to give back money because someone squirmed out."

"I'll be there," Gilmore snapped. "And I'll just put another twenty on my chances."

Ronsey looked over the barn and corrals. "Which horse are you racing?"

Gilmore swung his hand in a large arc. "He's down there," he said.

The arc included the corral and the barn. Ronsey and Tucker reined down to the corral and sat there, looking at the horses inside. It had to be obvious to Ronsey's trained eye that there was no special horse there. He turned and came back to Webb and Gilmore, confidence in his face.

"I'll cover your bet," he said to Gilmore. "I'll even make it higher if you're not afraid."

"Raise to fifty," Gilmore said without hesitation.

Ronsey grinned in satisfaction. "Everybody

here heard him. With the other fifty he bet with me and my boys, that makes a hundred dollars riding on the race." He leaned over from the saddle. "If you don't show up with your horse, you forfeit your bet."

"I'll be there," Gilmore said.

"Who's holding your money?" Ronsey asked.

"Webb," Gilmore said. When Ronsey frowned, he added, "Who's holding yours?"

"Quince," Ronsey said quickly. "If you don't pay off, I'll have your hide. Don't forget that."

He wasn't being so casual now.

"It ain't going to be me who'll be paying off," Gilmore said.

"We'll see about that," Ronsey said grimly, but there was satisfaction on his face as if he had just closed a very profitable deal. "Let's go, Quince."

The pair rode out of the yard, and Gilmore looked at Webb. "Suppose he does have a top racer?"

"Very likely," Webb said. "I know he's always challenged every newcomer to a horse race and I never heard of him losing."

"I told you he was here to see my racehorse," Gilmore said. "He didn't see him, though."

"I think he was here to size us up, too," Webb said. "He knows there are five of us. He saw you and Oldham last time. This time he saw Lon. He hasn't seen Brill yet."

"If Brill gets to him with that whip of his,

he'll wish he'd never seen him," Gilmore said, grinning. "I hope Peggy can win that race for us. I'd sure hate to have to pay off that skunk."

After Ronsey and his bodyguard were gone, Webb saddled up and rode west toward the herd. The cattle were on good pasture but were still being held in a fairly small area. Letting them scatter would just be inviting trouble if Ronsey's men decided to run off a bunch.

Everything was peaceful and Bruce Brill decided that Oldham might as well go back to the ranch. Brill, a real cattleman, wanted to stay with the herd and he was sure that, if trouble came, it would hit the ranch first. Oldham would be worth more there.

Webb had no argument for that, so he took Jay back to the ranch house with him, leaving instructions for Brill and Hank Masters to come on in to the ranch early the next morning. He figured that, if there was any trouble tomorrow, it would be in town. One man could watch the herd and the other the ranch house. Webb promised the hired hands extra pay for having to miss the celebration. He'd need all the hawks in town in case of trouble.

Peggy came out early on the morning of the Fourth to look at the horse again.

"I want him to be totally familiar with me," she said as she walked into the box stall with Blue Boy. He seemed as quiet with her there as he was with Gilmore. She petted him a little, then took him outside and rode him slowly around, getting the feel of the reins and how he responded.

"We'll give Dude a real race," she predicted as she left the barn. "I won't show up until time for the race. I don't want Dude to know I'm riding until the last minute."

Gilmore grinned. "And I ain't going to show Blue Boy till I have to. I might get some more bets out of Ronsey if he doesn't get a look at Blue Boy."

"It's no sure thing," Peggy said doubtfully. "Have you seen his racer? He bought him at a track back East. There hasn't been a horse come through here that had a chance with him until you brought this one."

"We'll win," Gilmore said confidently. "We've got to."

"How do things look in town?" Webb asked.

"Like a real celebration. Everyone has heard about the horse race and they're all talking about it. Two wagonloads of ranchers and cowboys came in from way over east last night. Guess there was nothing going on any closer, so they came here to celebrate."

"Do you think everything will be peaceful?"

Peggy frowned. "I hope so. I think Dude is so excited over this race that he won't cause any trouble."

"Even if he loses?" Webb pressed.

"I don't think he's considered that. We'd all better be alert if we do beat him."

Brill came in an hour later with Masters. That left Ike King watching the herd. Masters settled down to keep an eye on the ranch house while the others saddled up to head for Target. Gilmore decided to stay behind, bringing in Blue Boy just before race time.

Webb couldn't believe the race fever that had struck the little town. The cowboys from the ranches down the valley were all talking about the race. With the odds three to one in favor of Ronsey's racer, the cowboys made a lot of bets on Gilmore's horse, even though they had never seen him. Ronsey was in high spirits, just waiting to collect all his winnings when the race was over.

There were a lot of bets made on third place, since several cowboys had entered their horses. Few expected to place higher than third, figuring Ronsey's and Gilmore's horses had the first two places wrapped up.

Peggy was everywhere, it seemed to Webb, helping set up planks on boxes for chairs and tables for the big picnic dinner that would follow the foot races and precede the horse race. There weren't as many children as usual, but the cowboys and ranchers from down the valley had brought enough to make some lively running competition.

Ronsey had generously supplied a steer for roasting over an open pit. As Webb ate some of the beef, he wondered if it was one of his father's steers. Ronsey made no pretense of ranching, so he said he had bought the beef from a rancher.

Soon Ronsey came around to confront Webb. "Where is that horse that's supposed to give me a good race? If he doesn't show up, that money put up by your man is mine."

"He'll be here," Webb said. "And Ace Gilmore is not my man. He can take care of himself."

Ronsey grinned. "I see. You don't intend to be stuck with paying off his debt."

"Ever think that he might not have to pay off?"

Ronsey grunted. "He ain't going to win that race, that's sure."

Just then Ace Gilmore showed up, walking leisurely around the corner of the general store. Ronsey saw him and waited until he came closer.

"Where's your horse?" Ronsey asked.

"He'll be here when the race starts," Gilmore said.

"Who's going to ride him?"

Gilmore pursed his lips. "I may ride him myself if I can't find anyone else to do it."

Ronsey laughed. "That horse must be an elephant to hold you up and run, too."

Gilmore grinned. “No elephant. Just a faster horse than you’ve got.”

Ronsey’s face went livid. “You want to bet any more on that?”

“It runs me a little short on cash, but I’ll bet you another hundred.”

Webb interrupted. “Ace, are you sure?”

“I ain’t backing down,” Gilmore said.

Ronsey’s grin widened. “You’re on. I think that’s two hundred you owe me.”

“Not yet, I don’t,” Gilmore said.

Webb pulled Gilmore away from Ronsey before Ace bet the ranch on the race. Gilmore was a born gambler, but right now Webb was wondering how smart a gambler he was.

Then the dinner was over, and the excitement kept growing. It was time to bring out the horses for the big race. Peggy had disappeared right after dinner and now she reappeared with her hair done up in a bun and covered with a cap. She was wearing a divided skirt and carrying a small quirt. Webb stared. She looked just like a jockey.

Ronsey’s horse was already out on the road where a quarter of a mile had been measured off. Fad Vernon was in his glory. Riding Dude Ronsey’s racer was his only chance to be in the limelight. Webb had to admit that Ronsey’s racer was a fine-looking horse.

Gilmore came from Sid Cureton’s barn behind the store, leading Blue Boy. Peggy was boosted into the saddle and Blue Boy pranced out onto the road.

Webb glanced at Ronsey. The shocked expression on Dude's face, both at sight of the horse and the rider, was worth part of the money Gilmore had bet on the race. Fad stared at his competition, apparently realizing that, for the first time, he was going to have to work to win.

The horses headed for the starting line, a quarter of a mile from the crowd that was waiting to see the finish of the race. Ronsey rode beside Fad, talking in a low tone to him. Last-minute instructions, Webb guessed. Peggy didn't need any instructions, but Webb and Gilmore rode beside her to the starting line, anyway.

The starter lined up the horses. There were eight, counting the animals that the cowboys had entered. Still, to most of the spectators, it was going to be a two-horse race.

Suddenly Ronsey reined over to the starter, shouting that a girl could not ride in the race. Webb and Gilmore jerked their horses over to intercept him.

"Who says so?" Gilmore demanded. "There is no rule saying she can't. She's riding."

Ronsey swore but, looking over those who had ridden here to see the start of the race, he saw that opinion was against him. Growling curses, he reined off the road as the starter lined up the horses again.

Blue Boy appeared as eager for the race as Peggy. Webb had never before been this excited about a horse race himself. It would be a great day for Peggy and for Gilmore if they could win.

Then the gun popped and the horses lunged away from the starting line. Most of the riders who had come here to see the start kicked their horses into a gallop, paralleling the course. The course was a straight line and they had to hurry if they wanted to be close enough to see how the race ended. Webb and Gilmore were in the vanguard of those trying to follow the race, but they couldn't keep pace with the racers.

Ronsey's horse, having raced so many times, got the jump and took the lead. But Blue Boy was only half a length behind, matching the other horse stride for stride. Webb felt Gilmore's money slipping away. Blue Boy wasn't gaining.

Then, halfway to the finish line, Blue Boy did begin to gain. He was back only by a neck now. Inch by inch he crept closer.

Then it happened. Fad, seeing he was going to lose, brought his quirt around at Peggy. At the same time, he reined his horse toward Blue Boy.

VI

Webb yelled, but in the noise of the crowd the sound was lost. He saw Peggy dodge Fad Vernon's quirt, but the action made her jerk the reins on the horse, and Blue Boy broke his stride.

However, in his effort to push Blue Boy off his pace, Fad jerked his own racer to one side and he broke stride, too. Both riders swung their horses back on the racecourse. Blue Boy recovered quicker than Ronsey's racer and took the lead. When the two horses leveled out on the road again, Blue Boy was almost a full length ahead of his rival. The other horses in the race were so far back that the little ground they had gained by this disruption was barely noticeable.

Webb was running his horse parallel to the racecourse, trying to be close enough to see the finish of the race. He heard himself yelling like a madman, but again the sound was lost in the screaming of the other spectators. Peggy was far enough ahead of Fad now that there was nothing Fad could do to stop her. Blue Boy crossed the finish line a full length ahead of Dude Ronsey's racer.

Webb had to rein up before he reached the finish line because of the crush of the crowd. Fad's quirting of Peggy was close enough to the finish line for all the spectators to have seen it.

Dude Ronsey started charging toward Gilmore and Webb as soon as Blue Boy had won the race. Brill and Oldham were already with their partners.

"You cheated!" Ronsey shouted before he reached Gilmore.

"We cheated?" Gilmore screamed. "How about that jockey of yours trying to whip my jockey with his quirt. He ought to be shot."

Ronsey ignored Gilmore's outburst. "You didn't let me see your horse before the race."

"I didn't get to see yours, either," Gilmore shot back. "You and your friends owe me some money!"

"I'm not paying on a crooked bet," Ronsey snapped.

"If there was anything crooked, you did it," Gilmore shouted. "Pay up or I'll take it out of your hide."

Ronsey glanced back at Quince Tucker, right at his elbow. But Oldham, Brill, and Webb were backing up Gilmore. Dude's glance raced around the crowd. There was no question of the feeling of the people. Those who had come in from the ranches were definitely favoring Gilmore. Even Ronsey's own townspeople were reluctant to back Ronsey's claim, especially after the quirting incident.

Ronsey's face turned a dull red and sweat

popped out on his forehead. He was used to having his way and, this time, he could see that he wasn't going to get it. He looked around again. Webb looked, too, expecting to see Kurt Sikman and Tullie Cureton. But neither was in sight. Maybe they didn't like the odds against Ronsey.

Ronsey dug into his pocket and came up with a roll of money. He counted a few of the bills and threw them at Gilmore. Then he wheeled his horse with an oath and rammed his way through the crowd. Oldham picked up the money as it fluttered to the ground.

"Don't think he was too happy about that," Brill said, watching Ronsey leave.

"He'd have been a lot unhappier if he'd tried to weasel out of it," Oldham said, handing the money to Gilmore.

Webb felt it was time to head for home. But the hawks had different ideas. There were to be fireworks tonight and they didn't get to see fireworks often. Webb reluctantly agreed to stay.

During the rest of the afternoon, Webb and Brill stayed close to Gilmore. Webb suspected that Ronsey might order his men to retaliate for his humiliating defeat. The ranchers who had backed Gilmore on a hunch were celebrating over the sizable bets they had won. It had been a bad day for Dude Ronsey.

Lon Fleming circulated through the crowd, apparently not recognized as one of the hawks.

He brought word to Webb that three men were following them wherever they went. Webb watched and singled the three out of the jostling crowd. There weren't so many people in town; it was just that there was such a small area to hold the crowd.

When darkness began to fall, Fleming and Oldham joined the others and they formed a guard around Gilmore. Gilmore, the compulsive gambler, was difficult to shield. He wanted to get into some games, but Webb talked him into holding on to his money. A game would be a good chance for Ronsey's men to get back at him.

Peggy Cureton and Elizabeth Pinburg found a place close to Webb and his men for the fireworks display. Webb wondered if they were watching someone or if Peggy felt more secure close to the hawks. After all, she had ridden Blue Boy to victory. Ronsey wasn't likely to cheer about that.

The fireworks started and Webb kept one eye on the brilliant display and the other on the men he had been watching. They had moved up close behind them and Webb signaled Oldham. Webb turned suddenly and faced the three men.

"You boys want something?" Webb asked quietly.

Surprise hit the three men. Apparently they had felt that they hadn't been noticed as they followed Gilmore around.

"We—we're just watching the fireworks," one of them said.

"Do it somewhere else," Webb said. "We don't like to be crowded."

Consternation flushed their faces. Webb thought for a moment that they were going to fight. But they backed off and went farther down the street to watch the aerial display. Webb was convinced he had averted a nasty confrontation. They had probably planned to rob Gilmore or maybe even kill him. It convinced Webb that Ronsey was not going to take any defeat without striking back.

As the fireworks ended, Peggy and Elizabeth approached Webb. "Is our dance still on out at the ranch?" Peggy asked.

Webb shrugged. "Sure, if you can keep it peaceful after what happened today."

"I think we can guarantee that," Elizabeth said. "Pa and Mr. Cureton will help keep a lid on things. Some ranchers from down the valley will be there, too. A lot of them are here for the celebration. We want to get the invitations out tonight."

"And we'd like to come out soon and do some decorating," Peggy added.

Webb figured the girls meant they would like to come out and clean up the house. No doubt they wouldn't be too thrilled with the way it looked now, even though Webb and the hawks had swamped it out following the occupation by Ronsey's men.

"We won't object to that," Webb said.

"We'll be out in a day or two to start work," Peggy said.

Webb got his men out of town as quickly as he could. He and Bruce Brill rode in front and he told Gilmore to stay between Fleming and Oldham just behind them. Gilmore was surrounded. Webb imagined that Ronsey might have a price out on Gilmore's head. Gilmore had not only won a fair amount of money from Ronsey, but he had humiliated him and his horse today.

There was no threat made against them on the way home and Webb hoped the incident was closed. It had been a good day for them.

Things were quiet all during the next day, and even Gilmore was lulled into a false sense of security.

Two days later, Peggy and Elizabeth Pinburg came out to turn the house into an acceptable condition for the dance. It was scheduled for Saturday night. Gilmore took advantage of that time to give Peggy twenty dollars for riding his horse to victory.

Peggy objected. "That's a fortune!" she exclaimed.

"Takes less than half a minute to earn that much riding a winner," Gilmore said. "But you earned it. I got as much satisfaction out of seeing Ronsey eat dirt as winning the money."

"I was going to beat Fad even if he hadn't tried to hit me with that quirt," Peggy said. "Blue Boy was gaining on Dude's horse with every jump. The farther we went, the bigger the margin would have been between us."

"Is Fad that mean a man?" Webb asked.

"He's not mean at all," Peggy said. "I'm sure he had orders from Dude to keep me from passing him any way he could. Dude must have told him to hit me with a quirt, knowing I'd jerk my horse off stride. He hadn't figured on Fad's doing the same thing to his horse."

"What is Ronsey doing now?" Webb asked.

"Nothing," Peggy said. "Pa hasn't gone to any new meetings. But that worries me more than if I knew Dude was planning something in particular."

Webb agreed. When the girls went back to town, Webb went with them. He wanted to see for himself how quiet the town was. Brill insisted on going along and they rode partway up the street from the general store and looked around the corral next to the livery barn. Nothing seemed amiss. The town was quiet.

"Maybe Ronsey got a lesson that he'll take to heart," Brill suggested.

Webb shook his head. "Ronsey won't give up. He kept pushing us and our neighbors until the neighbors left. Then when my folks wouldn't leave, they were killed."

"You sure Ronsey did it? Could have been some rustlers who wanted the rest of your stock."

"I intend to find out," Webb said. "But we don't dare relax while Ronsey controls this town."

"Then we should all come in and clean it out," Brill said calmly.

Webb shook his head. He could see that Brill was serious. All the hawks would be in favor of that, except Fleming. They felt they had nothing to lose and plenty to gain if the area was rid of Ronsey.

"The Curetons are nice people," Webb said. "I wouldn't want to cause them trouble. I'm not sure about the Pinburgs. If those two families weren't in town, I'd favor a fight to throw out the whole outfit."

"Things sure look peaceful now," Brill said.

"Knowing Ronsey, that worries me," Webb said. "Maybe they just want to keep the lid on things till after the dance."

Suddenly Webb's attention was jerked to the north end of town where the doors of the saloon had burst open. Fad Vernon ran out, holding his hands over his head. Just two steps behind him came Dude Ronsey, a belt in his hand raised to strike at the boy.

Webb's reaction was instant. He wheeled his horse and kicked him into a gallop toward the saloon. He yanked out his gun and fired a shot well above Ronsey's head. Ronsey stopped as if he'd hit a brick wall. Fad came running up to Webb. Ronsey took one look at Webb, with his gun in his hand, and wheeled back into the saloon.

"What was that all about?" Webb asked Fad.

"He was going to beat me."

"Why?"

"I guess I earned it," Fad said. "I forgot to feed Mr. Ronsey's horse."

"He'd beat you for that?" Webb demanded.

"He beats me for anything," Fad sniffled. "I thank you for saving me this time."

"Will he whip you when you go back in there?"

Fad looked perplexed. "I don't reckon. Mr. Ronsey got a bad temper, but he gets over things fast. He's sure to beat me again when I do something bad, though. I sure won't forget you for saving me like this."

Fad turned back and walked slowly toward the saloon. Webb thought that he made a pathetic sight. He wished he could give Ronsey a beating for every time he had beaten Fad.

Webb turned to find Brill sitting close by, his gun in his hand and his eyes on the saloon.

"Ready to go home?" Webb asked.

"I ain't sure," Brill said. "I'd like to get a shot at Ronsey. I wish I'd had the chance you had.

I wouldn't have wasted that first shot by firing over his head."

Brill turned his horse back down the street and they rode out of town and back to the ranch. As far as Webb was concerned, he hadn't learned anything. He was puzzled by the total lack of activity in town. Ronsey was planning something—he was sure of that.

The girls came out again the day before the dance and brightened up the house with a final scrubbing and some fancy "doodads"—as Brill called them—strung across the walls. The place looked more like a ballroom than a ranch house when the girls went back to town.

Webb had talked to both girls about the way things were in town. They agreed nothing was happening and they were sure most of the townspeople would be out for the dance.

Webb checked the pen that held the goat. Dynamite stayed calm when nothing disturbed him. Yet, with so many people coming, he was bound to get excited. Fleming suggested with a grin that, when it was time for the dancers to go home, he might slip outside and release the goat. He was sure the dancers would all be gone in a matter of minutes.

Some of the ranch people from down the valley arrived late in the afternoon for the dance. Others came later and all the townspeople came at once, it seemed. The house and yard were full.

Webb saw several men that he knew from town and a lot of men he didn't know. He saw Tullie, as surly as he'd been the last time he'd seen him. He would bear watching. Sikman was here and Webb trusted him even less than he did Tullie. Even Dude Ronsey had come, but he appeared as gentlemanly as a Sunday-school teacher.

Before the dance got under way, Sikman went outside and, a couple of minutes later, Tullie went out, scowling as if he'd eaten a sour pickle. Webb didn't know what to make of that.

Then Fleming struck up the fiddle and the dancing began. Webb considered himself lucky to get Peggy for his first partner. He then danced with Elizabeth Pinburg. Both girls were having a grand time.

Then Webb got in line to dance with the other women, mostly wives of ranchers and of the cowboys from the ranches. The evening moved along rapidly, and Webb found himself relaxing. No trouble had erupted, and it appeared that none would.

Webb got a second dance with Peggy. She was bubbling with excitement over how well things were going. Webb was joining in her enthusiasm when he happened to drop his eyes and they fastened on the locket Peggy was wearing.

He'd have known that locket anywhere in the world. It had belonged to his mother. How did Peggy get it? He had been so sure that, when he found that locket, he'd find the murderer of his mother. Peggy Cureton was no killer, so that exploded his theory.

Clint was so shocked at sight of the locket that he lost track of the call and turned the wrong way in his square. Peggy caught him and turned him back. But he couldn't concentrate on a dance now.

The dance came to an end, and Clint pulled Peggy to one side, taking her away from the man who was waiting to claim her for the next dance. Webb was just ready to explain his impolite action when a man burst through the crowd around the open door. Webb was startled by the commotion. He shot a look that way and recognized Hank Masters, who had been out with the cattle herd.

"The herd has been stolen!" Masters yelled.

VII

If someone had thrown a stick of dynamite into the room, it wouldn't have caused any more confusion. The ranchers in the crowd suddenly remembered they had left their own cattle practically unattended. Though it was nearing midnight, when the food would be served, most of the men loaded up their families and headed for home, many miles away.

Webb made a quick survey of the crowd. He was willing to bet that this raid had been made by the same men who had stolen the cattle from these pastures before Webb's parents were killed.

He saw Dude Ronsey in the crowd. He wasn't surprised. Even if Ronsey was the boss of the rustlers, he would make sure he was seen here so he couldn't be accused of the theft.

Webb looked for other men from town. Sid Cureton was here; so was Norm Pinburg. Webb doubted if they had ever participated in a raid. But Webb couldn't find either Tullie Cureton or Kurt Sikman. He hadn't seen either of them since they had left the house just before the dancing started.

A few of the faces he had seen that first day—right here in this house—were here now. But not all. Clint guessed that some of those men had helped run off the herd.

Tucker was with Ronsey. That wasn't surprising. Dude Ronsey could run into trouble here if the hawks decided he was to blame for the rustling. Besides, Tucker was a bartender, not a cowboy.

The dance was over. All the food that had been prepared for eating at midnight was left on the big table along one wall. Webb made his way over to Hank Masters. As he got close, he saw blood on Masters's shirt.

"Did they shoot you?" he asked.

Masters shook his head no. "Surprised me. Hit me on the head with a gun barrel and knocked me off my horse. Then they stampeded the herd to the north and followed it. A couple of steers stepped on me."

"How about Ike King?" Webb asked.

"He was in camp. They didn't see him. I left him there to watch the stragglers that they didn't get."

"We'll go after the cattle and bring them back," Webb said.

"The rate they're going, they may run for ten miles."

Webb turned to the people still milling around the room. Picking out the hawks, he called to them to meet him outside.

"I'll take care of this man's sore spots," Peggy

said at Webb's elbow. "You go after that herd. I hope you can catch the thieves."

"They'll be traveling fast if we don't," Webb said. "Thanks for looking after Hank. Too bad this broke up your party."

"We had a wonderful time while it lasted," Peggy said. "Getting people to take home all that food may be the big problem."

The hawks reached Webb and he led them outside. Before Webb said anything about his plans, Brill spoke up.

"Better leave one of us here to watch the house. No telling what those skunks might do if we all go chasing after the rustlers."

"Good idea," Webb said. "How about you, Lon? You don't like riding too well and this could be a long, hard trip."

"Glad to stay," Fleming said. "I'll keep two rifles loaded and a couple of six-guns handy."

"We'll ride out to the bedding ground," Webb said. "We'll try to pick up the trail from there."

"Might be hard to do in the dark," Gilmore said.

"Maybe not," Brill argued. "Hank said the rustlers stampeded the herd to the north. A stampede usually leaves a plain trail."

By the time they had caught their horses and saddled them, most of the dancers had left. Only one buggy and a few horses were left in the yard. Lon Fleming was bidding everyone good night, making sure they all knew he was going to stay on the ranch while the others went after the rustlers.

Webb led out to the west. Brill, Gilmore, and Oldham were right behind him. He doubted if they could recover the cattle. Nobody had ever been able to find the cattle that has been stolen before. They had trailed the animals to the edge of the sandhills but had soon lost the trail. Nobody really wanted to go into those hills unless it was absolutely necessary. Since this herd had been stampeded to the north, they likely were headed for the hills, too.

It had been the theory of the ranchers that the rustlers had taken the herds only into the fringe of the hills and drove them east or west, then back out on the plains and to market. There were buyers who weren't particular about brands or previous ownership. With forged papers the buyers could ship the cattle to Omaha or Chicago and sell them to the slaughterhouses there.

The hawks reached the bedding grounds sometime after midnight. Webb rode slowly over the grounds before Ike King came up.

"Got a few strays down in a little draw," King said. "About all we have left."

"Did you see where the cattle went?"

"Sure did. I was asleep when they hit, but that stampede sounded like thunder in a rain barrel. They lit out to the north."

"Hank said he thought they might run for ten miles."

"I doubt that," King said. "They're pretty gentle cattle. But they would run far enough that nobody here would have a chance of catching up with them."

"Except the rustlers," Webb said.

"They went with them," King said.

"Can we follow them?"

"For a ways, I reckon," King said. "They went straight north. But if the rustlers turn the herd, we won't be able to find the trail in the dark."

Webb nodded and rode out to the north over the course that the cattle had run. Even in the starlight the trail was plain here. But a quarter of a mile ahead it became dimmer. Webb guessed that the cattle had spread out more, and the less-trampled grass was not so obvious in the dark. He turned back to the men waiting with King.

"Looks like we'll have to wait till we can see," he said. "It must be well past midnight now. Won't be long till dawn."

"Sure hate to let them get any more of a start," Gilmore said.

"I'd hate to get lost in those hills," Brill added. "I hear it's a death trap in there."

"We'll follow those cattle wherever they go," Webb said. "We're going to get them back. A couple of you ride back to the ranch and get some grub. We may be on the trail two or three days. No sense starving."

Gilmore and Oldham headed back to the ranch while Webb and Brill stayed with Ike King. They stretched out on the grass and tried to sleep. The other two came back before dawn with a flour sack full of food.

As soon as the light was strong enough to see the trail, the four men mounted their horses, leaving King to care for the few cattle they still had. The trail was easy to follow and by the time they had reached the point where it began to spread out and fade, the light was strong enough to show the signs well.

The trail led north, growing wider and dimmer as it went. Then, before they reached the sandhills rimming the north side of the valley, the trail turned abruptly to the east.

The sign was not so clear here, but the stolen herd was a big one. That many cattle had to leave evidence of their passing. The men rode rapidly until they reached the valley where Broken Horn Creek ran out of the hills toward the Platte River. Here the trail turned north directly into the hills.

They followed until they began to get into the sandhills; then Brill called a halt.

"We're taking a chance if we go any farther," he said. "I've heard about these sandhills. They reach for miles and miles in every direction. They say the hills are bare sand back a ways and the blowing sand can just bury a man."

Oldham nodded. "I've heard there's no grass there and no water. You notice there ain't much water in this creek here. It's spring-fed. Another mile and we'll hit the head spring. Then there'll be nothing. A man can die of thirst. And he gets lost just as soon as he loses sight of the plains. Many a man has died in there."

Webb could see that the hunt for the cattle was going to die right here if he didn't keep the men going.

"I've heard all those stories, too," he said. "My pa was afraid to go into these hills. So were his neighbors. But look at the trail. The cattle went in there. And you can bet the rustlers went with them. We can go anywhere the rustlers can go."

"Bet they turn the herd one way or the other before they lose sight of civilization," Oldham said.

"If they do, then we'll do the same. We'll follow the herd wherever it goes. We've got to get our cattle back."

The men nodded. Finally Brill, who was accepted as spokesman for the hawks, made his decision.

"I reckon I'm as tough as any rustler. I can follow any place they can go."

Webb led the way deeper into the sandhills. He couldn't help looking back and feeling a chill of apprehension when he could no longer see the flat land of the valley. His fear of the hills had been ingrained in him, but he wasn't going to let that stop him now. Buying the land of the three ranches would be a waste of money if they couldn't keep their cattle on it.

The trail led up the valley, turned into another valley between high sandhills, then turned again. Webb could see how it would be easy to get confused here. There was no way anybody could go in a straight line. Sandhills always blocked the path. The only way a man could get into the region was to follow the deep valleys, and these twisted and turned in every direction.

He didn't see the bare sandhills he had expected. There was an occasional blowout where the wind had whipped the sand away, tearing the grass out by the roots and leaving a deep sand bowl.

But, where the sand hadn't blown out, the grass was good. Even more surprising to Webb were the little lakes of water he found in the bottoms of some of the valleys. These sandhills were not a death trap. They were a wonderful pasture for cattle, though finding the cattle in here would be the drawback. A cow could be within fifty yards of a man and he wouldn't be able to see it.

Concentrating on the trail, Webb followed the stolen herd up one valley into another and then into another. If it hadn't been for the sun, he'd have had no idea where he was going.

The grass became heavier and the trail dimmer. Whoever had stolen the cattle surely knew where they were going. Twice the hawks lost the trail and had to backtrack to find it. Going back was a ticklish job. It could have been easy to turn down a wrong valley and they'd never have found the trail again.

It was near sundown when they turned up a valley and saw the cattle ahead of them. Webb reined up quickly and motioned his men back out of sight. The pocket where the cattle were being held was completely ringed by steep sandhills except for the open end where Webb and his men were.

"How many rustlers are there?" Brill asked when they were out of sight of the herd.

"We'll find out," Webb said. "You watch the horses and the rest of us will climb this hill where we can look into the valley."

They dismounted and Webb led Gilmore and Oldham up the steep side of the sandhill that formed one side of the pocket. Webb made sure that no one in that pocket could see them. He and his companions looked around carefully. Webb saw two men were with the herd. And after some searching, Gilmore located two more men in a tiny camp close to the mouth of the valley. Only four men.

Webb guessed this was where the stolen cattle from the valley had always been brought and held while new brands healed. Then they could be driven out to market. Nobody had ever followed the rustlers in here before; they obviously hadn't expected it this time.

Webb led the way back to Brill. They decided to wait until the next morning to strike. They had to see which way they were going when they took the herd back or they'd never get out of this maze of sandhills.

They made a cold camp. Toward daybreak, Webb decided he had to check once again to see how many men were in the rustlers' camp before they struck. Leaving his blankets, he crept toward the pocket.

There was a small fire at the camp not far from the mouth of the basin. There were just two men and he recognized one as Tullie Cureton. Both men were out of their blankets and, in a minute, Webb saw why. Two men were coming in from the herd. One was Kurt Sikman and the other a man Webb didn't know. Tullie and his companion rode out to circle the herd.

Webb realized there was no way the hawks could surprise all of them. They'd have to attack the camp and grab the men there, then go after the two with the herd.

While Webb was considering the best way to sneak up on the camp, he suddenly felt something prod him in the back.

"Don't move or you're dead," a voice said.

Involuntarily Webb turned to see what was behind him. The gun in the man's hand roared, but Webb had thrown him off balance by his quick move. The man soon righted himself, but by then Webb had his gun out and he slashed it down across the other man's arm. The man's gun went flying.

Jamming his gun in the stranger's middle, Webb ordered him back against the hill where they were out of sight of the little camp. Guns erupted at the camp, but the men were shooting blindly. Webb ignored them and made the man run back through the narrow valley. He found the three hawks up with guns in their hands.

"No sense in waiting now," Webb said. "This gent fired his gun and every rustler out there is aware that we're here. Saddle up. Let's go."

Oldham was assigned to watch the prisoner. No one had ever seen him before. Webb had questions he wanted to ask him, but he had no time now. Webb, Brill, and Gilmore rode hard toward the basin. But now they found the camp deserted. A gun roared over on the far side of the pocket. Dawn was bright enough now to show four riders forcing their horses up the steep hill.

"They ran," Brill said in amazement.

"Probably didn't know that there were only four of us," Webb said. "I thought there were only four of them, but here was a fifth one. Let's start the cattle toward home. We can see well enough now."

The cattle were milling, excited by the gunshots. It was no problem to get around them and head them out of the pocket the way they had come in.

On the way out of the basin, they picked up Oldham and his prisoner. Webb assigned Oldham to bring up the rear, keep the prisoner, and watch for any attempt by the rustlers to retake the herd. He sent Brill up ahead of the herd to watch the sun and point the way south. Gilmore and Webb drove the cattle.

It was afternoon when they broke out of the hills. Webb saw that they were to the west of the valley where the herd had gone into the hills. That put them close to their own ranch.

Some distance ahead, Webb saw a rider turn their way. Webb thought he recognized Dude Ronsey.

Dropping back till he met Oldham bringing the prisoner, he instructed Oldham to take the prisoner in a circle to the west and on to the ranch, making sure Ronsey didn't see him.

Riding back to Gilmore, Webb pushed the cattle on toward the ranch. Ronsey intercepted the herd and reined up. Webb rode over to him.

"Bringing in more cattle for your ranch?" Ronsey asked in a tight voice.

“Just bringing back what was stolen from us,” Webb said.

He watched Ronsey’s face, but it remained a rigid stare that would have done credit to a poker player. Webb would bet, though, that Ronsey knew exactly where these cattle had been.

VIII

Dude Ronsey sat quietly on his horse as he watched the herd of cattle stream past him toward the ranch pasture. He held his poise although he was seething inside.

This was the first time anyone had found his hideout in the sandhills. People were afraid of those hills, and Ronsey had done what he could to promote that fear. But these hawks and Clint Webb didn't react like any men Ronsey had ever dealt with. They seemed to have no fear of death.

Hundreds of cattle had gone into those sandhills and stayed there until new brands had been burned into the hides and the brands had healed. Ronsey had known when he first came here that if he didn't remove those ranchers, especially the Webbs, eventually someone would see some cattle going up that valley. So he had removed them, one way or another.

Now these new men had come and they had followed the first herd stolen and brought it back. They knew Ronsey's secret. His operation was doomed unless he got rid of those five men on the ranch and did it right away.

It had been Kurt Sikman who had brought him the report on what had happened back in the hills. At first Ronsey couldn't believe his bad luck. But fury had gradually replaced his feeling of shock.

Getting his horse, he had ridden out on the prairie to get his thoughts straightened out and decide what he had to do. It was pure chance that he had happened to be near the sandhills where the herd came out.

His first thought had been to hurry back to town for Quince Tucker. Ronsey very seldom rode anywhere without his bodyguard. Tucker was fast and accurate with a gun and was big enough that he could bluff any man who wanted to use fists. But today Ronsey had wanted to think and he hadn't wanted anyone with him.

Quelling his misgivings, he had ridden up and accosted Clint Webb, pretending he knew nothing about the stolen cattle. He was sure that Webb hadn't fallen for that, but Clint wasn't the kind to start shooting until he was certain.

Now Ronsey had to figure a sure and safe way to eliminate the opposition. What to do wasn't so hard to decide; how to do it was the problem. He had thought that, if the old men lost their cattle, they might give up and clear out. Instead they had gone right after the cattle and brought them back. And, in doing that, they had uncovered his secret of the sandhills.

Kurt Sikman had told Dude they had lost the stolen herd and blamed Tullie Cureton for being careless. Maybe he was right. Somebody certainly had been careless. When Ronsey got back to town, he'd find Tullie and see what he had to say about it.

He'd call a meeting of all the men in town and he'd assign jobs and they had better do what they were told to do. He rode back to town and put his horse in the livery barn where Sikman took care of him. Then he went down the street to Sid Cureton's store, looking for Tullie.

Tullie wasn't there, so Dude told Sid about the meeting at sundown at the saloon. Sid looked pale and old and Ronsey wondered if he was going to break under the strain. He couldn't depend on Sid for anything important, but he needed a storekeeper in town.

Outside, Dude ran into Tullie coming toward the store. He stopped the young man.

"What happened out there at the hideout?" Ronsey demanded. "Kurt said you were careless."

Tullie swore. "I was in with the herd. If anybody was careless, it had to be him. He was at the camp at the mouth of the pocket. That's where the ruckus started."

Ronsey merely nodded and told Tullie about the meeting at the saloon at sundown. Then he moved on. He'd decide who had been careless later. He thought that they had probably both been careless. He was aware of the rivalry between the two. Both wanted to be top dog with him, and he hadn't allowed either to claim that spot. Both were good with a gun, and he needed them both. Especially now.

For the game was over. He had pretended to accept the newcomers and it had worked to the extent that Webb and his men hadn't guarded their herd well. So the rustlers had made off with it without a hitch. The hitch had come later. Now it was open war until they got rid of those five men.

Dude went over to Pinburg's store and told Norm to be at the meeting. Pinburg wasn't any more enthusiastic about it than Sid Cureton had been. But Ronsey had both of them owing him favors, and they were making a good living here. If they had a lick of sense, they wouldn't tip the buggy they were riding in.

As the sun sank below the horizon, Ronsey went over to the saloon and on to his office behind the bar. His living quarters were behind the saloon, and Tucker had his own little room behind the office.

Sid Cureton was the first man to appear at the meeting. He took a chair back against the wall, as far from Ronsey's desk as he could get. It was obvious that he wished he wasn't there.

Norm Pinburg was the next and he sat back with Cureton. Sikman arrived, and then Tucker came in. The latter had turned the bar over to Fad Vernon, who enjoyed being bartender. Tullie was the last to arrive. He slumped in a chair close to the desk.

Ronsey turned to Tullie and Sikman. "You know you made fools of yourselves," he said in a low voice. "You destroyed our whole operation by letting those men find our hideout. Once they found it, your job was to make sure none of them got out of the hills alive. So what did you do? Ran like a bunch of whipped coyotes!"

Ronsey pinched his lips shut. If he said any more, he might break up the gang. He was furious enough to kill the ones responsible, and he blamed both Sikman and Tullie. There had been three of his cowboys with them, but he didn't expect cowboys to be leaders. They'd fight if they had a leader. His leaders had turned out to be cowards.

"We had no idea how many men were out there," Sikman said finally. "We figured it could be a sheriff's posse."

"Out there?" Ronsey exploded. "How long has it been since you've seen a sheriff or any other lawman near Target?"

Sikman looked at his feet. Tullie lifted his head and stared at Sikman, apparently pleased that he had been slapped down. Then Ronsey turned on him.

"You were out in the basin, Tullie. You had a good chance to see how many men you were facing. All you saw was the escape route up the hill. You must have located that long ago."

Tullie scowled and refused to look at Ronsey.

"All right," Ronsey said. "What's done is done. Now we've got to straighten out what we've messed up. We have to get rid of those five men before they tell some lawman what they have found out. You could have prevented all this if you'd taken the herd east and brought them back over that thick grass to the hideout. But you left a trail a blind man could follow."

"Nobody ever followed it before," Sikman said.

"You're not dealing with scared ranchers now," Ronsey said. "These men aren't afraid to die. So you have to kill them; you can't scare them away. I figure Clint Webb is the key to those men. He knows the country and now he knows how we operate. If we get him, the others shouldn't be so hard to handle."

Sikman lifted a hand. "I'll take care of him," he said.

"I can do it," Tullie said quickly.

Sid Cureton, who usually didn't say a word in these meetings, suddenly spoke up. "Let Kurt do it."

Tullie leaped to his feet. "Keep out of this, Pa. I can do the job better than Kurt."

Kurt Sikman grinned at the argument between father and son. But then Ronsey, quickly assessing the situation, stepped in. Sid Cureton was a nobody, but he was one that Ronsey couldn't fully trust. Now he thought he saw a way to keep him in line.

"Tullie gets the job," he stated.

Tullie threw up his hands in victory, not so much because he wanted the job, Ronsey was sure, but because he had beaten out Kurt Sikman. Sid Cureton slumped in his chair, totally defeated. Ronsey told himself he needn't worry about Cureton anymore. He had complete control over the man.

Sikman's reaction to Ronsey's decision was predictable. He was furious, more at Tullie's antics than at Ronsey. Ronsey knew Sikman felt that this relegated him to second place in the hierarchy and he wouldn't take that without a fight. Ronsey felt satisfied. Sikman had been too complacent, thinking he was second in command. Now he would have two hardworking men vying for the top spot, each trying to outdo the other.

Tullie strutted around as if he had just been made king. Ronsey was disgusted, but he knew that, after this demonstration, Tullie would feel compelled to make good on his assignment.

One question had been nagging at Ronsey ever since he had thought of it. Sikman had said two men had come back with Tullie and him. He hadn't mentioned the third man. Mose Yoder had been up in the hills with Tullie and Sikman and the other two hands.

"Did Mose Yoder come down from the hills with you?" Dude asked Sikman.

Sikman squirmed. "Mose was the one who alerted us to the trap," he said. "Tullie just took off and kept running. I circled back to get Mose, but he wasn't there."

"How did he alert you?" Ronsey demanded.

"Fired a shot. I thought maybe he had killed someone, and I went back to see and to get Mose. But he was gone."

"Where?" Ronsey demanded.

Sikman shrugged. "Since I couldn't find hide nor hair of him, I figure the old men captured him."

Tullie was on his feet. "I didn't run as fast as Kurt did," he shouted. "And Kurt knows what happened to Mose. We both saw him being taken back with the old men as they drove the herd out of the hills."

Ronsey felt the pulse throbbing through his head. "You saw him and you didn't make any effort to get him back?" he screamed. "I ought to shoot you both. I will shoot you if you don't get him back tonight. He knows too much about things. They might make him talk. I'm giving you both the job of getting Mose away from them. If you don't do it tonight, you won't live to see another sunset."

"What if they have him guarded so we can't get to him?" Sikman asked.

"You get him. That's an order! If you see you can't, then shoot him. He can't be allowed to tell what he knows."

Ronsey saw that his orders were a bit shocking to the others but he made no further explanation. None of them knew what Mose Yoder knew about Ronsey's past. If Yoder told what he knew, it could mean that Ronsey would go back to prison in Ohio for the rest of his life. Ronsey considered Yoder a good friend; that was the reason he had trusted him never to tell what he knew. But he couldn't let friendship stand between him and prison.

Ronsey dismissed the meeting, and Sid Cureton and Norm Pinburg were the first ones out of the room. Sikman and Tullie were still sparring. They shared the assignment of freeing Mose Yoder, but Tullie had the plum assignment of getting rid of Clint Webb. That put him a step above Sikman and he wasn't letting Sikman forget it.

Sikman made it clear that he didn't think Tullie was man enough to handle the job Ronsey had given him. "Dude should have sent a real man to do that job," he said.

Ronsey saw that the argument between the two was getting out of hand, and decided to step in. But before he could put that decision into action, Sikman called Tullie a name that he wouldn't take. Tullie reached for his gun. He was a good shot but not extremely fast in handling a weapon.

Sikman was both fast and accurate. Both guns roared, but Sikman's was first and he was the only one standing when the smoke drifted away.

Ronsey let out a yell. He felt little remorse over Tullie's death, but he was furious that one of his own men had thinned his ranks. Ronsey needed every man he had. Those old-timers and Clint Webb were much more formidable foes than he had expected.

His first impulse was to grab his own weapon and gun down Sikman. But now that Tullie was gone, he'd need Sikman more than ever. Besides, he probably wasn't fast enough to beat Sikman. If he had to eliminate Sikman, he'd assign the job to Quince Tucker. Nobody Ronsey knew could beat the bartender with a gun.

Dude felt half-naked with one less gunman around him. He thought of bringing up one of the men down in the camp. But their job was rustling cattle. They were paid well for that. He couldn't afford to make any changes.

"Now, Kurt, you'll have to do both jobs yourself," Ronsey growled when he had control of himself. "Get Mose free, then take care of Webb. I want both jobs done as quickly as possible."

"Sure," Sikman said. "You saw Tullie. He drew first."

"You opened your mouth once too often," Ronsey said. "From now on, try to keep it shut unless you've got something worth saying. The next time you open it, you can tell Sid Cureton that you killed his boy. Do that right now."

Sikman scowled, but he left the office. Ronsey checked Tullie's body. As he had expected, Sikman's shot had been dead center. He left the office and walked down to the hardware store. Norm Pinburg was in the front of the store, looking up his way.

"I heard a shot," Pinburg said when Ronsey came inside.

Ronsey nodded. "Sikman called Tullie a raw name and Tullie drew on him. Kurt was too fast. You're the one who takes care of funerals. Go up and get Tullie."

"Have you told Sid yet?" Pinburg asked.

"I told Sikman he had to do that. He's the one who killed Tullie."

Ronsey wheeled out of the store. He'd made all the arrangements. Walking back to his saloon, he watched for Sikman. Would he tell Cureton as he'd been ordered to do? Tullie had drawn first, but Sikman had provoked him. Ronsey himself would have gone for his gun if anyone had called him a name like that.

Sikman came out of the livery stable on his horse and rode down the street. Deep dusk had settled over the street now, softening some of the harsh features of the town. It was a pretty valley, Ronsey thought as he watched Sikman. Even the town was rather pretty. But what was going on here wasn't pretty. Ronsey's little paradise was tumbling down. If Mose Yoder talked, it would come crashing down in a heap.

Ronsey felt sure Yoder wouldn't talk, but he'd also been sure those old men weren't much of a threat. Ronsey scowled as he saw Sikman ride right past Cureton's store and keep on going. He wasn't following his orders to tell Sid about Tullie. What else would he skip?

Ronsey hurried across the street and got his horse. He rode slowly along the road toward the Platte River. Sikman was going that way, not toward the ranch where Mose Yoder was being held. Maybe Sikman was running out. If so, Ronsey would shoot him before he got to the river.

But Sikman stopped at the camp below town where Ronsey's men were staying. Ronsey stopped well back from the camp where the darkness hid him. He had to see what Sikman was up to.

In fifteen minutes, Sikman rode back out of the camp, and he had a man with him. Ronsey sat his horse quietly, waiting until they were close enough that he could see who it was. When he saw, he understood. The man Sikman had brought with him was Mose Yoder's best friend. Ronsey saw through Sikman's strategy. This man would go to greater lengths than anyone to rescue Yoder. Ronsey liked Sikman's plan.

Still, he followed them as they rode slowly to the west toward the ranch. Would Kurt Sikman go on with the man? Or would he send him in alone where he stood a good chance of getting caught or killed?

A quarter of a mile from the ranch, the two horsemen ahead of Ronsey stopped. Ronsey reined up to wait and watch. Finally, one rider went on ahead while the other stayed and watched him go. It was Kurt Sikman who had stayed behind.

Ronsey had to admire the way Sikman handled things, letting someone else do the risky work to save his own hide. Now came the question as to whether it would work. Ronsey guessed it was more likely to work with Yoder's friend trying the rescue than it would have with Sikman doing it. Sikman would be more likely to kill Yoder since he wouldn't care that much whether Yoder lived or died.

Ronsey reined his horse around toward town. Things could get sticky out here if that man ran into trouble. Ronsey didn't want to get involved. He had to trust Sikman to handle things if the other man couldn't do it. If Ronsey was going to get into it, he wanted Quince Tucker with him. Maybe he should have sent Quince after Yoder. He'd have done the job some way.

But he had sent Sikman. Now he had to accept the outcome.

IX

Webb was weary when he and the men got the cattle back on the grass west of the ranch house. Gilmore was ready to drop, but Brill seemed able to stand up to the work and said he'd stay with the herd until the cattle had settled down.

After riding back to the house, Webb and Gilmore took care of their horses and went inside to rest. Oldham was there and had his prisoner tied to a chair. Hank Masters had recovered enough from his injuries to go out and help guard the herd. Webb didn't expect another raid on the cattle. Now that the rustlers' hideout had been discovered, they would have no place to take stolen cattle for rebranding.

Lon Fleming, who had stayed at the ranch while the others had gone after the stolen cattle, said he wanted to ride out to the herd. He'd been cooped up too long.

"Better watch that goat," he warned as he was leaving the house. "He has been mighty restless ever since the dance here. I saw him butting the fence as if he thought he could tear a hole in it."

"He might do it," Webb said. "That pen was built for calves, not goats."

Webb was too tired to worry about Peggy's goat or even the prisoner. He'd query him later.

He just wanted to stretch out now and rest. He doubted if the rustlers would rest as long as the hawks were headquartered this close to the trail into the hills. Only now did he realize that that had been the motive behind the harassment and murder of ranchers near the town.

Now that Webb and the hawks were here, they would be even less acceptable to the rustlers than the previous ranchers had been. They would also be much harder to dislodge. If Ronsey was the head of the rustlers, then he must also be the boss of whoever had murdered Webb's parents.

Webb intended to find out not only who had masterminded the murder but also who had done the actual killing. Making them pay for the crime wouldn't bring his parents back to life, but letting the killers run free to kill again was unthinkable.

Webb dropped off to sleep going over the suspects: Dude Ronsey, Quince Tucker, Kurt Sikman, and Tullie Cureton. Those were the main ones.

A yell brought Webb out of his sleep. It was late afternoon, but he was sure he'd have slept another five hours without waking if it hadn't been for that yell.

Grabbing his gun, he ran to the door. Oldham and Gilmore came, too. Lon Fleming was in the yard, attempting to head off the billy goat, which was trying to dodge past him.

Webb shoved his gun back in the holster and

hurried out into the yard. Fleming was going to need a lot of help to head off that goat.

"Open the gate," Webb yelled at Gilmore. "We'll try to herd him back into the pen."

"Won't do any good unless we fix that hole," Gilmore said. Nevertheless, he opened the gate into the pen and stood back to help drive in the goat.

The goat had other ideas and a few men were not going to change his mind. Fleming was talking soothingly to Dynamite after the others came to help him thwart the goat's escape. The goat backed off, shaking his head as a warning not to crowd him.

"You can't soft talk a billy goat," Oldham yelled. "You got to show him who's boss."

He picked up a stick and made a pass at the goat when the goat tried to dodge past him. The stick slapped against the goat's horns as he ducked the blow.

The goat didn't stop; he simply changed his direction from the gap between Oldham and Webb to a beeline toward Oldham. Oldham had no chance to escape the goat's charge. Dynamite caught him in the middle and butted him backward. He landed hard on the seat of his pants and skidded a couple of feet. The goat stood back, shaking his head.

Webb moved over quickly in front of the goat to prevent him from continuing his attack. Gilmore and Fleming came running to form a close half circle around the creature.

Dynamite looked defiantly from one to another of the men, then backed off a few steps, still not turning around.

"We have to coax him back into the pen," Fleming said. "You see what force does to him."

"I've got a six-gun that will change his mind," Gilmore said.

"This isn't our goat," Webb said quickly. "He belongs to Peggy. You wouldn't want to kill her goat, would you?"

Reluctantly Gilmore shook his head. "She won me some good bets. I guess I can put up with her goat for a while longer."

Oldham got gingerly to his feet. "If he belonged to anybody but Peggy, I'd settle his hash right now," he growled.

Webb knew that Peggy was the sweetheart of the hawks. They'd do almost anything for her, but he wasn't sure how much longer they would tolerate her goat.

Fleming had the best luck of moving the goat in the direction they wanted him to go. He talked softly and coaxed the animal back toward the pen. Once they got him inside the pen, Gilmore raced over to block the hole where Dynamite had gotten out. Ace wasn't a minute too soon. When the goat realized he was back in the pen, he made a run for the hole where he had escaped before. But Gilmore was there and he had a crude club. The goat was smart enough to know he had no chance against that club as long as there was a fence between him and the man with the weapon. He shook his head furiously but he backed off.

It took the men half an hour to mend the fence, and Webb wasn't sure then that it would hold the goat. Now that Dynamite had found out how to get out of the pen, he'd surely try the same tactics again.

Webb went back into the house where the prisoner they had captured up in the sandhills was still sitting in the chair where they had tied him.

"Have you decided to talk to us yet?" Webb asked.

"I ain't squealing on nobody," the man said.

"What's your name? That wouldn't be squealing on anybody."

"Yoder," the man said.

"Who do you work for?"

"Who said I work for anybody?" he snapped.

"You weren't up there for your health," Webb said. "Somebody was paying you to guard those cattle."

"You're so smart, you figure it out."

"Let's take him out and put him in the goat pen," Gilmore suggested. "That billy goat might butt some sense into him."

Webb grinned. "It just might, but he might not be able to talk when the goat got through with him. We'll just keep him tied to the chair. He'll get hungry pretty soon. And he might get tired of sitting on that chair."

Yoder scowled at the men, but he didn't say a word.

"What does Dude Ronsey have to do with the rustling?" Webb asked.

Yoder looked sharply at Webb, but he said nothing.

"I take it from what you're not saying that Ronsey is the ringleader of the rustlers."

"You can make up all the lies you want to, but you won't prove anything that way."

Webb knew the man was right. But he thought that in time Yoder might tell more.

He left the man in the chair and went into the other room with the others following. The men were almost ready to go to bed when they heard a commotion outside. A bleat of the goat alerted them to the nature of the trouble.

"That goat is out again!" Oldham shouted. "Let me kill him this time."

"It's Peggy's goat," Webb reminded, knowing that would quiet the threats against the goat.

They ran for the door as the commotion out in the yard increased. Just as Webb burst out the door, he heard the fence squeal like a rabbit caught in a trap. It was fairly dark in the yard, but Webb could see the white coat of the goat squeezing out of his pen.

There seemed to be a purpose in the goat's movements. Then Webb saw the man. He had been sneaking toward the house but now, with the goat charging toward him, he wheeled and ran for a horse beyond the corral.

Just outside the corral was a windmill that Webb had helped his father put up over a well. A pipe ran from the mill to the tank, which was half in and half out of the corral, so water could be taken from the tank on either side of the fence.

The man apparently saw his mistake only after he had started toward his horse. The pipe to the tank was between him and the horse at the far side of the corral. He made the only choice possible. He headed toward the pipe, apparently with the intention of jumping over it.

The goat wheeled toward him and rapidly closed the gap between them. Webb was amazed at how fast that goat could cover ground. The man was just starting to jump over the pipe when the goat reached him. With horns lowered, the animal caught the man in the seat of the pants. Dynamite was just enough to one side to change the man's direction as his feet left the ground. The intruder went headfirst into the tank, slipping under the fence that bisected the tank and ending up sputtering in the corral half.

Webb reached the fence, ignoring the goat, and

yelled for the man not to move. He jerked out his gun and aimed it at him. It wasn't too dark for the man to see the gun. He meekly held up his dripping hands.

"What kind of a skunk did you catch this time?" Gilmore asked.

"Probably somebody coming to get our prisoner," Webb guessed. "Am I right, mister?"

"I sure wasn't coming for any stinking goat," the man muttered.

"Get out of that tank," Oldham ordered. "You're smelling up the water. Then climb over the fence where we can get a good look at you."

While the man obeyed the orders, Fleming began talking softly to the goat, coaxing him back toward his pen.

When the man reached the outside of the corral, Webb took a good look at him. He might be one of the men who had been in the house when the hawks had run Ronsey's men off the ranch.

He saw that Fleming was having good luck returning the goat to the pen. He assigned Gilmore to stay and help Fleming fix the fence again as soon as they could get the goat inside the pen. He and Oldham took their new prisoner into the house. The man still dripped water from his dunking in the tank.

"Did you ever tease that goat?" Webb asked when they got in where the lamp was burning.

The man was surprised at the question. "I hate

all goats," he said. "If that is Peggy Cureton's goat, I've tangled with him before. He hates me."

"They say a goat never forgets anyone he don't like," Oldham said.

"I didn't know the pest was here," the man said. "He saw me before I saw him."

"Who sent you here?" Webb asked.

The man pinched his lips together before he answered. "I came on my own," he said finally.

"Did Ronsey send you?" Webb pressed.

"No," the man said quickly. "Dude wouldn't send a man near a place where that goat is. He's teased that goat more than anybody and the goat really hates him."

"If he didn't send you, who did?" Webb demanded.

"I told you, nobody sent me. I heard that Mose Yoder was here and I came to get him. He's my friend."

"That's more than you can say for the goat," Oldham said.

"I could take you out and put you in the pen with the goat if you won't talk," Webb said.

"Ain't nothing to talk about," the man said. "I came to get my friend, but I ran into the goat instead."

Webb believed him. But it increased his curiosity about what Yoder knew that was so important. He waited till Fleming and Gilmore came in, then held a private conference with the three hawks. He wished Brill was here, but he was still out with the herd.

They decided they had gotten everything out of this man that they were going to. So they freed him, telling him they would hold Yoder till he told them what he knew.

Once the still wet, uninvited guest had hurried out to his horse and disappeared into the night, Webb turned his attention once more to Mose Yoder. He must know something important. But Yoder was adamant in refusing to talk.

"You deny that you work for Ronsey?" Webb pressed.

"I ain't talking about Dude," he said.

"How many cattle have you helped drive into the hills?" Webb asked.

"I don't keep count of the cows I trail."

"Does Ronsey pay you well for what you do?"

"I don't go hungry," Yoder said.

It was the most Webb had gotten from Yoder. He interpreted it to mean that Ronsey was his boss and he was paid well for what he did. More questions brought little else from the prisoner.

Webb called the three hawks into another room to decide what to do with Yoder.

"Unless we torture him, he ain't going to talk," Gilmore said. "We can't spare one man just to guard him."

"You're right," Oldham said. "We've all got

better things to do than sit and look at his ugly face."

Yoder was wide-eyed with surprise when he was released.

He had barely gotten out of sight in the night when Webb announced that he was going to town. It wasn't too late and there were things he needed to find out. He'd go alone. If anybody went with him, there would be more chance that they'd be discovered.

Clint was tired, but he kept thinking about that locket Peggy had been wearing at the dance. He hadn't had a chance to ask about it then—Masters had broken up the party by shouting that the herd had been run off by rustlers. Webb had to find out where Peggy had gotten that locket.

The town was quiet when he arrived. There were lights in the saloon and in Pinburg's house. Cureton's store was dark, but there was a light in the living quarters above the store.

Dreading what he might learn, Clint tied his horse behind the store and quietly climbed the outside stairs to the door. He hoped Peggy wouldn't say she got the necklace from her father. He knew that Sid Cureton was involved in some way with Ronsey, but he was not the kind of man Webb could picture as a murderer.

Sid Cureton answered Webb's soft knock. Surprised, he invited him inside. Webb saw that Winona Cureton and Peggy were both still up.

Everyone was subdued and the women had been crying.

"Something wrong?" Webb asked, forgetting for the moment about his mission.

"Kurt Sikman shot Tullie," Sid said. "We knew Tullie was running with the wrong crowd, but we never thought it would come to this."

"Sorry to hear that," Webb mumbled, surprised and embarrassed. "Maybe I'd better go."

"Wait a minute," Peggy said. "You must have some reason for coming this late."

Webb glanced around at the three mourners. "I just wanted to know where you got that locket, Peggy. That was my mother's locket, and she never went anywhere without it. I figure she was wearing it when she was killed."

Peggy gasped. "I never suspected it had belonged to her," she said. "Pa gave it to me for my birthday."

That was the news Webb had been afraid of. He saw Peggy's face mirror his thoughts.

"You don't suspect Pa of killing your parents, do you?" There was accusation and almost hysteria in her voice.

Webb shook his head hastily. "No, of course not. I just need to know where he got it."

"I bought it from Quince Tucker," Sid Cureton said quickly. "He said he bought it in Denver."

"Do you believe that?" Webb asked.

"Up till now, I had no reason to doubt it," Sid

said. “Do you think Quince could have been the one who killed your folks?”

“I sure intend to ask him,” Webb said.

Before he could ask to see the locket, a knock hammered on the door. Webb wheeled that way. Someone must have seen him come up here. If it was one of Ronsey’s men, that could mean trouble for him and for the Curetons. And who else but one of Ronsey’s men would be in town?

Webb knew that all the Curetons must be thinking the same thing he was.

“I’ll have to see who it is,” Sid said, starting toward the door.

X

"Wait a minute, Pa," Peggy said softly, stopping her father. "They must be after Clint. I'll take him down into the store and let him out the back."

Sid Cureton nodded as the knocking got louder on the door. Webb followed Peggy to the stairway down into the store. Quickly they descended, and Peggy unlocked the back door. Webb stepped outside. Above, in the living room of the Curetons', he heard loud voices. Whoever had come inside was demanding something. He heard Sid almost yell that Peggy was in bed and he wasn't going to wake her up. He saw Peggy fade into a dark corner of the store where he knew she would stay until the visitor was gone.

Webb ran to his horse, which was only a few yards away. He swung quickly into the saddle and walked the horse quietly out on the grass behind the store. Only when he was some distance from the building did he put the horse to a trot and then a gallop toward home.

He believed Sid Cureton when he had said he'd bought the locket from Tucker. The Curetons had proved to be as friendly toward him as they dared to be while living in Ronsey's town. Maybe they had overdone it a little tonight. Clint was grateful to them for slipping him out. It had surely saved a gun battle. He knew that Ronsey wanted him dead.

In Webb's mind, Quince Tucker was guilty of the murder of the Webbs until proven innocent. He'd face Tucker at the first opportunity and give him a chance to explain how he got the locket. But he wouldn't accept any lies.

When Webb got home, he found that Bruce Brill had come in from the herd. Everything was going well there and Brill wanted a bed to sleep in. Webb himself was dog tired. His nap this afternoon hadn't been long enough.

Webb was recovered by morning and the others seemed to be, too. Gilmore and Oldham wanted to go to town. Webb advised against it. He expected Ronsey to order his men to eliminate any man from the ranch. Gilmore and Oldham agreed but felt they could do some eliminating themselves if it came to a fight.

When the two saddled their horses for the ride into town, Brill got his horse, too. There was strength in numbers, Brill said. After they had disappeared, Webb decided he'd better go, as well. He wanted to face Tucker and demand an explanation about the locket. If there was strength in numbers, one more should help.

Fleming asked if he should go and Webb suggested that he stay and watch the ranch. There was always danger of Ronsey's men simply slipping back in. Then things would be back where they had started.

Webb rode into town, expecting to find Gilmore and Oldham in the saloon. They both loved to gamble. He was surprised when he passed the Curetons' store to see Gilmore, the real gambler, there. But Webb's target was Quince Tucker and he kept riding toward the saloon.

Brill was just going into the saloon as Webb tied his horse at the hitchrack out front. Brill had his big whip wrapped around his wrist, the way he carried it when he was expecting trouble. He could flick a fly off the wall with that whip and he could draw his left-hand gun with reasonable speed if the whip couldn't do the job.

Webb stepped inside. The saloon was almost empty. Norm Pinburg was there instead of tending to his hardware store. He was in a card game with Jay Oldham. Oldham was frowning when Webb first saw him. A second later, Oldham jumped to his feet, knocking his chair backward.

"You're cheating, Pinburg. I won't stand for that."

Webb had started toward Tucker, who was behind the bar. Now he jerked his attention to the argument at the card table. Pinburg was also on his feet but not reaching for his gun. He shot a look at Tucker, then looked back at Oldham, denying that he was cheating.

Webb guessed that Pinburg had been cheating.

Oldham wouldn't deliberately pick a fight with Pinburg, who was no threat to the hawks.

Suddenly Pinburg reached for his gun. Oldham was watching for that and drew his gun much faster than Pinburg. Oldham's shot nicked Pinburg's gun arm and the latter dropped his gun. Webb guessed that Oldham hadn't meant to kill the hardware man.

But Webb's attention was jerked away from that fight as Tucker came around the corner of the bar in a blaze of speed for a man of his size. He had a gun in his hand. But Brill, who had been standing back as a spectator, suddenly snapped his whip. The lash snaked around Tucker's wrist, flipping the gun to the floor.

Tucker swore, looked at Brill, saw that he had no gun in his hand, and stooped over to scoop up his own gun. That was the moment Brill flipped the whip again. This time the lash cut a slice of the ample seat of Tucker's pants.

Tucker straightened with a scream that surely must have been heard all over town. Pinburg was standing near the card table, one hand holding the arm that had been nicked with Oldham's bullet.

"Get out of here, Jay," Brill shouted. "I'll be right behind you." He looked at Tucker. "Don't reach for that gun again or I'll cut out a chunk of hide as big as your bottom."

Tucker glared at Brill, breathing hard. Webb

knew he was hurting but, after that one scream, he wasn't making a sound.

Oldham backed through the door and Brill followed him. Webb knew he was expected to go, too, but he had come to corner Tucker and demand some answers. He'd never find Tucker as helpless as he was right now, so he stayed.

The moment the door closed behind Brill, Tucker reached down for the gun again. This time Webb stopped him. He had his gun trained on the big bartender.

"Don't touch it, Tucker," he said. "I've got some things to discuss with you."

Tucker straightened up again, glaring at Webb. "What about?" he growled.

Webb shot a glance at Pinburg. He was no threat although Webb could see that he wasn't hurt much.

"I've been told you sold a locket to Sid Cureton. Where did you get it?"

"What locket?" Tucker growled.

Webb stepped closer to Tucker. "You know what locket I'm talking about. Where did you get it?"

Tucker retreated. "I got it in Denver."

Webb studied the bartender's fat face. He was lying. He'd stick by that lie if Webb didn't force the truth out of him. He took two quick steps that brought him face to face with Tucker. Then he jammed the gun into his fat belly. Clint knew he wouldn't have much time to get a confession out of Tucker. That shot would bring somebody to investigate.

"I'm telling you, I—" Tucker began.

"I want the truth!" Webb snapped, jabbing the gun harder into Tucker's yielding belly.

The color drained out of Tucker's face. Maybe it was fear that Webb would shoot. But Webb thought it was more likely fear of what Webb would do after Tucker told him where he really got the locket.

But Tucker was rescued by the sound of a horse's sliding feet at the front of the saloon. Footsteps hit the wooden porch. There was a back door right at the end of the bar and Webb gave the gun a shove into Tucker that brought a gasp from him, then ducked through that door before the front door opened.

Webb's danger was smothered in his frustration. He had come within a few seconds of getting the truth out of Tucker. He was sure of that. Maybe he should have killed Tucker for the murder of the Webbs. But what if he wasn't guilty?

Webb had to admit he was speculating. He couldn't kill a man on speculation. He had to know he was right. He wondered who had charged up to the front of the saloon. In Target, it had to be Ronsey or one of his men.

Webb lost no time in getting around to his horse in front of the saloon and racing out of town. Not until he was well away from the buildings did he relax. He had cut it mighty thin.

At the ranch, he found all the hawks there. Brill and Oldham had come straight home and they had picked up Gilmore as they left town.

"What happened to you?" Brill demanded. "You were right there when we left."

"I had a talk with Tucker, but somebody came charging in. I had to leave before I found out what I wanted to know. I'm almost convinced that he's the one who killed my parents."

"Why didn't you kill him on general principles?" Oldham said. "You know he ain't fit to live."

"I want to be sure I get the right man," Webb said.

"Ronsey was probably in on it, but I'll bet he didn't do the killing," Oldham said. "Does that mean you're going to let him go free?"

"If I find out he ordered their murders, I'll settle with him. But until I know, I won't go after him."

"I don't figure you're going to have to go after anybody," Brill said. "They're going to come after us."

"If they do, we'll accommodate them. But we have to watch for tricks. We can't trust them."

"Imagine that little pip-squeak of a Pinburg cheating in cards," Oldham snorted. "If we can't trust Pinburg, there isn't anyone in town we can trust."

"I think I'd trust Cureton," Webb said. "But probably nobody else. From here on, we're going to watch them all as if they were enemies."

"Does that mean we aren't going into town anymore?" Gilmore asked. "That would be admitting they have us whipped."

"Not necessarily," Webb said. "We'll go in when we have to, but we'll be ready for trouble at the drop of a hat."

"I think we ought to challenge them," Oldham said. "We're not going to have any peace until we clean out that town."

"I agree." Gilmore nodded. "If we go in there like we're not afraid of anything and face them down, we might buffalo them."

"I doubt that," Webb said.

"There's got to be a better way," Fleming said. "If we use our heads, we might lick them without sending half of us to the cemetery."

"Does that mean you ain't willing to ride in with us and clean them out?" Oldham demanded.

"I didn't say that," Fleming said. "I just think we ought to look for a safer way to drive them out of the country."

"I'd rather drive them six feet under the country," Oldham grunted.

Webb asked for ideas from anyone, particularly Fleming, on how to cope with the men in Target.

Fleming said he'd think about it and give them a proposal soon. Soon wasn't quick enough for Oldham and Gilmore.

Just at sundown, a rider was spotted coming toward the ranch and he was riding hard. Webb studied him carefully. The others checked their guns. But Webb put them at ease when he identified Fad Vernon.

"Why would he be coming out here?" Brill asked. "He's Ronsey's errand boy."

"That could be exactly why he's coming," Webb said. "He may be running an errand for Ronsey."

The men left the house, peering cautiously in all directions. "Could be a trap of some kind," Oldham said. "Fad may just be a decoy."

Webb had thought of that and he was watching, too. The ranch house sat out in the middle of the bottomland and there was virtually no way to sneak up on it without being seen. That little knoll to the west, which Webb and the hawks had used when they first arrived, was about the only rise in the land near the house.

Everything appeared quiet except for Fad riding up to the hitchrack. He threw himself from the saddle and ran up to the men. He singled out Webb.

"I'm scared for Peggy," Fad panted.

"What about her?" Webb asked, gripping Fad's arm.

"Quince told Mr. Ronsey something about a locket, and Mr. Ronsey says he wants that locket right now. Quince said Mr. Cureton gave the locket to Peggy. The way Mr. Ronsey yelled, I'm scared something bad'll happen to Peggy."

Webb's heart chilled as he listened. He should never have said anything to Tucker about that locket. Most likely Tucker had taken the locket from Webb's mother and said nothing to anybody about it. Then he got the chance to sell it to Sid Cureton and make some money. Could Tucker possibly know the secret that Webb's mother said was hidden in it?

Webb put all that speculation behind him as he considered the threat to Peggy. Peggy might be in real danger. Besides, he certainly didn't want Ronsey to get his hands on that locket. Why did Ronsey want it? Did he know the secret in it?

"Thanks for riding out and telling me, Fad," Webb said. "I'll go in and talk to Peggy about it. Maybe she can get rid of it before Ronsey gets it."

"If Peggy gives it to Ronsey, she shouldn't be in any danger," Brill said.

"That locket was my mother's," Webb said. "If Peggy gives it to anyone, it's going to be me—if I can get to town in time."

"We'll ride along," Gilmore suggested.

Webb shook his head. "I think I'll have a better chance of getting that locket if I'm alone. Too many of us showing up in town could stir up a real fight and that wouldn't help Peggy."

The idea of hindering instead of helping Peggy carried some weight with the hawks and they reluctantly agreed to stay home. Webb saddled his horse quickly and rode back with Fad. It was dark when they approached town.

"You'd better disappear, Fad," Webb said. "You can't afford to be seen with me. I appreciate what you've already done."

Fad nodded and reined off to one side to ride in from a different angle. Webb was starting to rein in at the general store when he saw two people walking up the street toward the saloon. He nudged his horse forward and cut in front of them.

"Where are you going?" he demanded of Quince Tucker. Peggy was with him.

When Tucker didn't answer, Peggy did. "Quince said that Dude wanted to talk to me."

Webb watched Tucker. Clint had obviously taken him by surprise and his slow wit was finding it hard to plan his next move. Webb directed his next question at Tucker.

"What does he want with Peggy?"

Tucker shook his head. "I—I don't know."

"He wants her locket, doesn't he?"

Tucker's eyes popped. "How did you know that?"

Webb thought of challenging Tucker. But

Peggy might be hurt in a gunfight. He couldn't risk that. He checked Peggy's neck. The locket wasn't there. She apparently wore it only on special occasions and this wasn't one of them.

"You're wasting your time, Tucker," Clint said. "Peggy lost that locket."

While Tucker was absorbing that information, Webb swung off his horse. He stared at Peggy, hoping she'd go along with his lie.

Tucker stuttered a bit, then turned to Peggy. "Did you lose that locket?"

"Why, y-yes, I did. Is that why Dude wants to see me?"

"If you lost it," Tucker said, anger building in him, "you'd better find it 'cause Dude says he wants to see it, and he wants to see it tonight."

Peggy had recovered from her surprise. "Pa gave me that locket," she said spiritedly. "I don't have to show it to anybody."

Tucker was taken aback by her sudden defiance. Webb took advantage of his confusion to step in and take Peggy's arm.

"I'll see her home, Tucker," he said.

Quickly he started back down the street toward the store. He expected Tucker to challenge him, but apparently the bartender was too confused by the sudden happenings to think straight.

"What is this all about?" Peggy asked softly as they neared the store.

"Fad rode out and said that Ronsey wanted

that locket. It was my mother's, you know. She told me there was a secret hidden in that locket. I didn't want Ronsey to get it."

"What kind of secret?" Peggy asked.

Before Webb could answer, a shot roared from the corner of a shed north of the general store. Webb pushed Peggy to the ground while he dropped himself. Webb's horse jerked free and trotted around to the far side of the store. Webb tried to make out the figure at the corner, but he couldn't see him well enough to identify him. Webb's first thought was Ronsey. He must have been shadowing Tucker and Peggy to make sure the bartender got her. Now he was taking a hand himself.

"Run home," Webb ordered sharply. "I'll keep him busy."

Another shot came from the corner of the shed, barely missing Webb, who was flat in the dirt in the middle of the street. He had no protection here. The ambusher would get him if he had another shot or two.

XI

"Run!" Webb told Peggy again.

If Peggy stayed out here, she'd likely get shot, too. She took off like a racer, almost flying from a prone start. Webb fired two quick shots at the corner of the shed, not being particular whether he hit anything or not. He intended to make sure that the ambusher didn't get a good shot at Peggy.

Two more shots came from the shed. Both were aimed at Webb. He was rolling toward the far side of the street, not taking time to answer the shots. Another gun roared from a window above the store. Cureton had his head out the window yelling. He couldn't have known who was doing the shooting, but he was afraid Peggy would be hit. Evidently he knew she was out there.

Webb reached the far side of the street with only a scratch on one arm. He didn't know whether to credit the darkness with his good fortune or whether the ambusher was too eager to take time to aim carefully.

No more shots came from the corner of the shed and Webb dashed up the street. He was sure it must have been Ronsey shooting at him. Who else would know that Tucker was bringing Peggy to the saloon and who else would be so disturbed at Webb's interference?

Clint had known he was risking a battle when he came into town with Fad. But he couldn't let Dude Ronsey get his hands on that locket.

There was no one near the shed. Clint really hadn't expected anyone there after Cureton had fired that shot from the upstairs window. Webb looked behind the buildings and soon found himself up near the livery barn across from the saloon. If it had been Ronsey shooting at him, chances were good that he was back in the saloon now. Quince Tucker would be there, too, and maybe some more of Ronsey's crew. Webb would be a fool to go in there looking for him.

He found his horse standing, reins dragging, on the far side of the store. He knew it wouldn't be wise to hang around town. Either Ronsey or some of his men would surely come out looking for him. There was no doubt in Webb's mind that they intended to kill him if they got the chance. He was giving them that chance by staying here.

As he mounted, he thought of the locket. He had to find out the secret it held. But there was no light in the store or in the living quarters above it. Apparently the Curetons had gone to bed, hoping the trouble would go away. There had to be a better time to get that locket. Webb was running too great a risk by staying in town now.

Riding to the ranch, he found the place dark. He took care of his horse and slipped inside. Brill had fallen asleep in a chair, waiting up to make sure Clint got home all right. Webb slipped past him to bed.

Webb faced a disgusted Brill the next morning. He spent most of the night waiting for Webb, then woke up in the small hours of the morning to discover Webb in bed. During breakfast, which Fleming had cooked, Webb explained what had happened and finished with a warning that it was likely open warfare from here on in.

"This is a poor time for that," Fleming said. "We're short of supplies. We'll have to go to the store to get some."

"Bet Ronsey won't let Cureton sell us any," Brill said.

"I think Sid will sell to us," Webb said. "The question is, can we get into town and back alive?"

"I'd as soon take my chances on that as starve to death," Gilmore said.

They all looked at Webb. He was supposed to know what to do. This was his country. He made a quick decision. It was necessary that Fleming be one of the men to go because he did the cooking, so he'd know what they needed. Brill had the coolest head among the hawks, so Webb picked him to go with Fleming. Their orders were to slip into town—unnoticed if possible—get the supplies, and get out immediately.

Webb watched the two ride off. He had thought about sending them in a wagon so they could bring back a big supply of food. They had a good work team that his parents had left here, and there were two wagons. But a wagon was too noticeable and too slow in case they had to run for it. So all the supplies they could bring would have to come in saddlebags.

Webb expected them back by noon and it was almost noon before Bruce Brill showed up. Fleming was not with him. Webb was the first one into the yard to meet him.

"Where's Lon?" he demanded.

"Held in the saloon in town," Brill said angrily. "We were buying our supplies. We'd given Cureton the list and he had most of it gathered up. Then three men charged through the front of the store and another popped in the back door. Sikman was the only one I recognized. They held us at gunpoint."

"How did you get away?" Gilmore asked.

"They grabbed Fleming and turned me loose. I was to bring a message to Webb that they'd turn Fleming loose if Webb would come to the saloon."

"That's a trap if I ever saw one," Oldham said.

"Sure is," Brill said.

"What will happen to Fleming if I don't go?" Webb asked.

"They said they'd kill him. I figure they will, anyway. They're out to kill us all, I'm sure."

"We can't leave Fleming there," Webb said.

"I suppose you're going to be brave and sacrifice yourself?" Gilmore said.

"I'm going to do what I can to get Fleming free," Webb admitted.

"We've got to go in there with guns blazing," Gilmore declared.

"I figured we'd all go back in a bunch," Brill said. "I knew I couldn't do anything alone, especially while they were all watching me. So I came home and hoped somebody would have an idea we could use to get Fleming out of there."

"How many men do you think are in the saloon?" Webb asked.

"There were a dozen horses tied in front," Brill said. "I figure they were planning a raid on us. Then we walked right into town, so they changed their plans. They likely think if they can get rid of you, Webb, they can run the rest of us out of the country."

"I reckon they've got something to learn then," Webb said. "I haven't seen anyone here who is easier to push around than I am. I'll go and see what I can do."

"You can get killed, that's what," Brill growled. "If we all go, we'll be outnumbered about three to one. But at least we can take a few of them with us when we go. I say we make a charge at the saloon."

"That might be fun," Oldham said, his face bright with excitement. "But I ain't that anxious to die. I've got an idea. Maybe it ain't worth much, but I don't see how we'll lose anything if it doesn't work."

"Got a way to surprise them?" Gilmore asked.

"Sort of," Oldham said. "I was thinking of that goat. Dynamite hates me and I hear he also hates Ronsey and Tucker. Probably a lot of Ronsey's men have teased him, too."

"What are you getting at?" Webb pressed, thinking this might be leading up to something they could try.

"If we can sneak that goat into the saloon," Oldham said, eyes gleaming, "he'll make a mess of things in short order. It might give us a chance to knock off a few of them while we get Lon out of there."

Webb considered the outlandish plan. As Oldham said, they weren't likely to worsen their position by trying. It just might work.

"How do we get that goat near the saloon?" Gilmore asked.

Webb answered slowly, "You know Broken Horn Creek runs down the valley just behind the saloon and Pinburg's house. If we load the goat in his crate and put that in the wagon, then take a long loop around town and follow the creek bed to the back of the saloon, they might not see us. It's a long shot."

"That's better than charging straight at them," Brill said. "Let's try it."

“Can we get up to the back door of the saloon from the creek?” Oldham asked.

“It isn’t over ten yards from the bank of the creek to the back door. If nobody sees us out of the back of the saloon, we might make it.”

Webb knew the odds were against them, but the rewards of success would be worth the risk. He led the men into the yard.

Webb was glad now that he’d decided to leave two workhorses and a couple of wagons behind when he left the valley at the instigation of Ronsey’s men. Those horses and wagons were still here.

Hitching up the team of horses and pulling one of the wagons around to the calf pen, they contemplated their next job. They got the crate that the Curetons had used to bring the goat out to the ranch. Putting it up against the calf pen, they opened the crate, then opened the gate into the pen. The goat balked. He’d been in that crate before and he didn’t like it. They left Oldham to drop the door shut behind the goat if they got him in the crate, while the other three climbed into the pen.

They took some good licks from the goat before they grabbed him by the horns and dragged him, with one man pushing, to the crate. After they got his head into the crate, it still took a mighty shove by all three men to push him the rest of the way. Oldham dropped the door of the crate shut behind him.

Quickly they lifted the crate into the wagon. Webb took the reins and they began their long roundabout journey to town. Dynamite butted the end of the crate angrily. He was furious and Webb hoped he stayed that way till they got there.

Webb crossed Broken Horn Creek and went north, finally turning back to the west. Hitting the creek bed north of town, he turned south. There was only one window in the north side of the saloon and the wagon was hidden by the bank of the creek. If someone didn't go outside and look north, the wagon shouldn't be detected before it reached a spot directly behind the saloon.

Ronsey's private living quarters, at the rear of the saloon, were only half as wide as the saloon, so the men would have to go past them to reach the saloon's back door. Webb was betting that Ronsey wouldn't be back there this time of day, especially when they were looking for the hawks to come to rescue Fleming.

The wagon wheels squealed. It had been some time since they had been greased, but likely that sound, as well as the sound of the goat, would be drowned by the noise in the saloon as Ronsey's men waited. As they neared the rear of the saloon, Webb kept thinking of the many things that could go wrong.

But they reached the spot directly behind

the saloon without a challenge. The goat was still furious as they unloaded the crate from the wagon. Webb knew he'd butt them all over the place if he could only get out.

"Bruce, you carry the guns," Webb said softly. "If anyone sees us, we drop the crate and grab our guns. Bring a rope, too."

With Gilmore and Oldham on each side of the crate near the front, and Webb at the rear, they started the climb up the bank of the creek to the level land behind the saloon. Dynamite was heavier than Webb had expected, but they got him to the top.

They reached the back door of the saloon, just inches away from the side of Ronsey's living quarters. With a deep breath, the men set the crate down. Webb gathered them together to whisper final instructions.

"Tie your rope to his leg, Bruce. We have to let him out of the crate and pointed toward the door."

That was easier said than done, but the goat didn't make any noise other than sliding his feet as he was dragged out of the crate. Once he was out, Oldham stepped in front of him to kick open the saloon door. Dynamite made a lunge at him, but Oldham dodged and nothing but the open door was in front of the goat. Nobody had a chance to get the rope off the goat's leg.

Dynamite went through that door as if it were

the pearly gates to paradise. Webb got a look inside over the top of the goat. The men in the saloon had just wheeled around at the sound of the door bursting open. Ronsey was the nearest man to the back door. Apparently he had stayed behind his men as they faced the front where they expected an assault. The rear attack came as a complete surprise.

The goat must have recognized Dude Ronsey instantly as one of his tormentors from the past. He may even have blamed Ronsey for the recent humiliation of being shoved into the crate and jolted all the way to town, since Ronsey was what the goat saw at the moment. There was no doubt about his target the instant he got into the saloon.

Ronsey was not slow-witted. It took him no more than a split second to recognize his danger. He wheeled toward the front of the saloon, but that escape route was blocked by his own men gathered for the frontal attack. Spinning to avoid the goat, he made for the bar to his right. Quince Tucker was there, supplying the needs of a couple of the men waiting for the battle.

Ronsey almost made it to the bar when the goat caught up with him. Dynamite made a solid connection with Ronsey's rump just as the saloon owner started to jump over the bar. With the uplifting help of the goat, Ronsey cleared the bar by three feet and crashed full force into Tucker.

Bottles crashed and the shelf below the mirror gave way under the sudden weight of Ronsey and Tucker. Broken glass and whiskey exploded in all directions. Tucker clawed automatically for the gun under the bar and brought it out with a jerk. It crashed into the mirror and shattered it.

The goat, seeing his enemy disappear over the bar, wheeled toward the men who were staring in disbelief. Dynamite recognized enemies there and charged toward them. There was a stampede for the front door, but it hadn't been built for the passage of ten men at once. There was a jam at the door and the goat jammed it harder, like ramming a cork into a bottle.

Ronsey and Tucker finally got to their feet, slipping around on the messy floor covered with whiskey and broken glass. Webb was inside the saloon now with his gun in his hand. But neither Ronsey nor Tucker was showing any inclination to fight the white demon that had wrecked the place in a matter of seconds. They both dived out the side door before the goat could locate them.

The front doorway finally cleared, but the door itself was torn off its hinges. The goat triumphantly followed the men out into the street, precipitating a stampede down the street. The goat was doing a better job of herding men than any of the men could ever have done herding goats.

Sitting quietly in the center of the saloon—

because he was tied to a chair—was Lon Fleming. Webb hurried to him and jerked off the ropes.

"Let's get out of here before Ronsey and Tucker figure out that the goat isn't chasing them anymore."

They hurried out the back door and down the embankment to the wagon. Oldham and Gilmore brought the crate. That belonged to Peggy and Ronsey would destroy it if he found it.

Webb took the reins of the team and popped the horses into a good trot along the edge of the creek until they were well south of town. Then he pulled them up on the level prairie and headed them west to the ranch. As they passed the town, he saw horses scattered among the few buildings. The sight of the men charging out of the saloon with a goat on their heels had been too much for the horses, which had broken their reins and left the area in a hurry.

"Won't any of them be chasing us," Gilmore said. "Especially that one." He pointed to one man on the roof of a little shed behind the hardware store. The goat was just below him, shaking his beard angrily.

They reached home without incident and Webb felt that it had been a very successful trip indeed. None of them was hurt, they'd all had a good laugh at the expense of Ronsey's men, and, most important, they had rescued Fleming. Brill had been right. It had been a trap to kill Webb. Any one of the hawks attempting a normal rescue of Fleming would have been killed. Peggy's goat had changed that.

"Wish we had that goat back here," Gilmore said. "He's as good as a regiment of soldiers."

Later in the day, Peggy Cureton and her father came out to the ranch in a wagon. The billy goat was tied to the wagon and he was pulling back on the rope. Webb decided there was no giving up in that goat. He had been virtually dragged three miles from town and he was still fighting the rope.

"Can you put up with Dynamite a little longer?" Peggy asked when the wagon stopped. "If we try to keep him in town, Dude Ronsey will kill him. From what I hear, he gave Dude a pretty good wallop. And he scattered Dude's men like frightened quail."

Sid Cureton gave one of his rare smiles. "It may take Dude a week to round up all his men."

"That goat did better than a half-dozen gunmen," Webb said. "We appreciate getting him back."

Cureton drove the wagon close to the goat pen. "Here's your groceries, too," he added, handing Fleming a big sack. "You left in sort of a hurry and didn't take them with you."

Webb helped get the goat back into his pen,

then turned in time to wave at Peggy and her father as they moved the wagon back toward town. He wondered what Ronsey would do now. He hoped he wouldn't strike at the Curetons.

XII

As her father drove the wagon toward town, Peggy looked back at the men in the ranch yard. She wished she could have heard their version of what had happened at the saloon today. But her father wouldn't stop to visit. That might give Ronsey grounds to suspect they were siding with the hawks and Clint.

Peggy liked all the hawks and hated to think of anyone hurting them. She liked Clint Webb especially well, but she doubted if he thought that much of her. She certainly wasn't going to let him know how she felt.

She had known that Ronsey's men had kidnapped Lon Fleming. That had happened right in the store. She knew that Bruce Brill had been sent back to the ranch with a message for Webb to come in if he wanted Fleming released alive.

She had wanted to ride out to the ranch and see what Webb would do, but her father had absolutely forbidden it. If Ronsey found out she had gone to the ranch, he'd declare that her father was helping the enemy. It could cost him a lot, maybe even his life. So Peggy had stayed in the store and worried.

The first she had known of any rescue attempt was when men started exploding out of the saloon with Dynamite right after them. She had supposed the goat was back at the ranch in his pen. She called her father and mother to watch.

It took her no more than a few seconds to figure out what had happened. Obviously Clint and his hawks had let the goat in the saloon's back door. If he'd gone in the front, the men wouldn't have been coming out that way. She had enjoyed the sight of the men running in all directions. She saw one man pass the hardware store, then run along the side of the store to a little shed. For some reason, Dynamite had sorted him out of the bunch to chase. The man barely got on top of the shed before the goat arrived. Peggy was surprised that the goat hadn't jumped up there, too. He could jump a lot higher than that. But maybe there just wasn't room for both him and the man up there.

Peggy had seen the wagon come up over the riverbank south of town and go toward the ranch. The goat crate was in the back of the wagon. It didn't take a genius then to understand how the men had gotten the goat to the back of the saloon.

Peggy did wonder what had happened to Dude Ronsey and Quince Tucker. They had surely been in the saloon, but they hadn't been in the bunch that tore the door off the front getting out. They must have taken a side exit.

Peggy and her father had speculated gleefully on the way out to the ranch with the goat about what might have happened to Dude and Quince. The goat had finally calmed down and he had come right back to his usual stall. Peggy wanted to keep him, but she knew that now Dude Ronsey would kill him for sure if he stayed in town. She could imagine how the interior of the saloon must look after the goat had put those men out of there.

As the wagon rumbled back toward town, Peggy couldn't keep her mind off Ronsey. What would he do now? Her father had said that Ronsey had planned a frontal attack on the ranch and had brought in all his men from the camp down the creek. That's how they happened to be in town when Brill and Fleming came in for supplies.

They had obviously changed their plans when they got a captive and used him as bait to lure the other hawks into their trap. That trap had sprung in an entirely different way from what they had expected. So now would they go back to their original plan?

Peggy was glad that Ronsey hadn't asked her father to take part in the raid on the ranch. Still, he had been in on the plans. She knew her father didn't like what Ronsey was doing, but she also knew that he owed his good living to Ronsey and Ronsey held it over his head like a club.

The kidnapping had surprised her father as much as it had the two hawks. The direction of

Ronsey's thinking became clear, though. Brill had been instructed to tell them at the ranch that Fleming would be released if Webb would come in and get him. The trap had been designed especially for Webb, but it would spring on any of the hawks that showed up.

Peggy saw Ronsey at the front of the general store as they drove in. She guessed they were in trouble. Ronsey had a cut on his forehead and his hand was bandaged.

"What happened?" Sid Cureton asked as he stopped the team.

"That cussed goat of yours!" Ronsey roared. "I told you to get rid of him."

"We did," Cureton said. "We took him right back out to the ranch. They have a pen there that will hold him."

"Did they say how he got out?" Ronsey asked.

Peggy realized that all Ronsey had seen of the rescue attempt was the goat. Evidently he hadn't talked to any of his men yet. Or maybe none of them had seen anything but the goat, either. She could hardly hold back a smile.

"They didn't say a word about it," Peggy said. "They just put him back in the pen."

"If he shows up in town again, I'll kill him," Ronsey said. "You should have to pay for what that goat did to my saloon. Sid, you be at our meeting at sundown."

Sid Cureton groaned, but Ronsey ignored it as

he headed back up the street. Peggy knew how her father dreaded those meetings. She didn't know why Ronsey always included him, but he and Norm Pinburg always had to go, just as faithfully as Ronsey's gunmen had to. Perhaps Ronsey included them so they would know what would happen to them if they ever turned traitor.

"He'll probably accuse me of helping the enemy," Sid said as he took care of the team.

Peggy helped him, knowing how worried her father was. From the condition of Ronsey, she imagined his temper would be very short. She wondered exactly what had happened to cut him up like that, especially since he obviously had not tangled with Webb or any of the hawks. He didn't seem to know they had even been in town.

They finished caring for the horses and headed for the store. Fad Vernon was inside, perched on a barrel. Instead of resenting Peggy for beating him in that race on the Fourth of July, he seemed to be much more friendly than before.

"Did you see what happened in the saloon today?" Peggy asked him.

He nodded, eyes glistening eagerly. Obviously he wanted to tell what he had seen.

"Everybody was watching the street," Fad said. "Dude said he knew Clint Webb'd show up. He don't abandon one of his men. Then your goat bust in through the back door. He took right after Dude. The other men piled up in the front door so Dude had to scoot over the bar. The goat gave him a real thump over. Dude hit Quince and they bashed into the shelf and all the whiskey bottles—broke almost every bottle! Then Quince tried to grab his gun, but he jerked it back so hard it broke the mirror.

"Then the goat went after the rest of the men. They tore down the door hinges to get out. He chased them way off into the street."

Peggy was laughing. "We saw that, but we didn't know what happened inside. Where were you?"

"I was over at the side. Dude don't let me talk with the other men. The goat didn't even see me. He left Fleming alone, too. He was tied to a chair. Then Clint Webb come in and untied him and they went out back and took off in their wagon. It was some sight, the way that goat run everybody out of the saloon!"

At sundown, Sid Cureton headed for the meeting. Peggy's mother was fit to be tied. She insisted that Sikman should have been punished for killing Tullie, but Ronsey had done nothing. Ronsey had been pushing people around for more than a year now, and it was high time he was tarred and feathered and run out of town. The problem was that her husband would never do anything about it. So Winona was ready to take over the job. Peggy had enough of her mother's temper to agree that something had to be done, but Peggy insisted that it wasn't their place to do it.

Finally, Winona declared she would kill Ronsey if he gave Sid any more trouble, and Peggy could only calm her down by saying she'd go herself and try to eavesdrop on the meeting.

Shortly after her father had left, Peggy went outside and turned up toward the saloon. It was dusk but not dark enough to cover her movements. She crossed to hide behind the hardware store and move along to the rear of the saloon.

She had to slip around Ronsey's living quarters to the door where the hawks had released the goat. She could hear nothing here. Around on the north side of the building was the room Ronsey called his office. It had an outside window and there were no buildings north of it. Maybe they were meeting there.

She moved quietly up under that window. From there, she could hear everything that was being said. She couldn't always identify the voice, but she knew better than to lift her head to look.

She did identify Ronsey's voice, though, and he did most of the talking. He was sure that, if they could kill Clint Webb, the hawks would be easy to get rid of. Something had to be done. The hawks knew too much now. Besides, Ronsey couldn't have anybody living that close to his trail into the hills.

He said he wanted to be democratic and asked

for ideas on how to get rid of the five men on the ranch. Someone—Peggy thought it was Sikman—said they couldn't storm the ranch. Those five would surely kill several of them. They didn't seem to be afraid to stand and fight. That kind of man was dangerous.

"Kurt, it's your job to kill Clint Webb," Ronsey said. "I'm holding you to that."

"I want Brill," another voice said. "He cut me with that whip of his. I aim to kill him myself."

That would be Quince Tucker, Peggy knew.

She tried to listen to the rest of the plans, but she found it hard to clear her mind of Ronsey's determination to kill Clint Webb. That upset her more than the plans to kill the other four and she couldn't deny it.

When none of the men could agree on anything, Dude Ronsey announced a plan of his own.

"We'll steal the herd again," he said.

"We tried that once," Sikman shouted. "It didn't work. It won't work now. They know where we hold the cattle."

"Simmer down," Ronsey snapped. "I've got it figured how we can clean out that whole bunch on the ranch. There are still only two men guarding the herd, I hear. We can take care of them and get the herd. We'll leave a good trail straight north. The whole bunch should come after us. When we get in the hills, we'll cut them down. They won't expect more than four or five of us to be with the herd. We'll have fifteen or more."

"Where are you going to get that many?" Sikman asked. "That's more men than we have."

"We've got extra men here in town who can drive cows," Ronsey said. "Sid, you and Norm can help."

Peggy heard her father speak up for the first time. "What about our stores?" he asked. "Who's going to run them?"

"Your wives can keep the doors open if they want to," Ronsey said. "Just who do you think will be your customers when we have all our men out with the herd?"

"What if all the men out on Webb's ranch don't follow the herd?" one man asked.

"If we get Webb, the rest won't be hard to eliminate. Any more questions?"

Peggy waited, but she heard no other voices raised. As always, Ronsey's plans were adopted. He ruled the town and the men in it with an iron hand. Peggy knew how her father would hate this assignment. She had thought he might balk, but now she realized that Ronsey had a death grip on him. Whatever Ronsey asked him to do, he'd have to do it. Most likely he knew he'd be killed if he didn't.

"One more thing, Quince," Peggy heard Ronsey say. "You get that locket. I don't care how you get it, but get it."

Peggy caught her breath. She waited for her father to say something, but he didn't. He probably didn't dare raise his voice against Ronsey twice in one meeting. She had no idea what secret that locket held, but she was going to find out.

She slipped away from the window and hurried home. She told her mother simply that Ronsey was asking for plans to eliminate the men out on the ranch. She didn't tell her about the plan Ronsey had put forth.

Peggy had feared Ronsey was suspicious that the Curetons were helping the enemy. However, instead of dressing down Sid as she had expected, he had assigned him to help steal the herd this time. If he was one of the rustlers, then none of his family would dare tip off the hawks. Ronsey was devious, but usually successful. Peggy wouldn't dare warn Webb about the raid. That could lead to her father's death.

She slipped off to her room and lit her lamp. Then she dug down in her bureau drawer. She had hidden the locket there when she found that it was creating such a stir. She hadn't examined it inside except to see that it held a picture of Clint Webb's father. She hadn't recognized that picture until Webb had told her that the locket had belonged to his mother.

Peggy studied the picture now. Surely there was nothing in it that was valuable. She pried out the picture and found nothing behind it. After examining the locket on the outside for engraving or marks, she finally put it back. She'd let Webb find the secret if he could.

After supper, Sid Cureton said he was going to do an errand for Ronsey. He might be back tomorrow and he might be two or three days. Winona scowled but accepted the explanation. Peggy didn't. She realized that she must have left before Ronsey set a date for the rustling. Tonight was the night.

Sid Cureton went outside and saddled his horse and rode away. Peggy tried to think of some excuse to bring her father back. But she knew Ronsey would retaliate immediately if she did.

Peggy went to bed as usual, but she couldn't sleep. She had to do something. It went against her nature to sit back and let her world fall apart without trying to save it.

Suddenly she leaped out of bed and into her clothes, a new thought driving her. Maybe Ronsey planned to get rid of her father somewhere out in the hills. He could give any of a dozen explanations to Winona about how he got killed. Ronsey would secretly gloat that he'd gotten rid of a traitor.

Peggy had to get to her father and warn him about what she thought might be in the wind.

She rode hard toward the place where the hawks were keeping their herd but, when she got there, the cattle were gone. She guessed they had already been stolen and were probably up in the sandhills now. She hoped the hawks hadn't discovered the loss yet, but she guessed that the men with the herd had left to report to the ranch.

Peggy's main concern now was for her father. The more she thought about it, the more she thought that Ronsey might be planning to get rid of him. Ronsey wouldn't tolerate anything but total submission to his orders and he had reason to doubt her father's loyalty.

She headed into the hills. There wasn't much light, but she could see where the cattle had gone. She had heard Ronsey say they'd go straight north into the hills, leaving a clear path so the hawks would follow right into the trap.

Peggy was well into the hills, following the trail up a valley between high sandhills, when she heard a rumble like distant thunder. She scanned the skies. She could see stars. It couldn't be thunder.

Then, as the rumble rapidly grew louder, Peggy knew what it was. A stampede. She wheeled her horse but, even as she did, she saw through the dusky night the leaders of the herd charging around a hill directly at her.

The horse panicked and stumbled as he whirled and began running. Peggy knew that if he fell she would be trampled to death. And she could feel him falling.

XIII

Webb had been driving his horse hard, hoping to catch up with the rustlers who had stolen the herd. All the hawks were fuming over this second attempt to steal their cattle. They were determined to punish the thieves this time, whatever Webb might say.

It had been just bedtime when Ike King and Hank Masters had come charging up to the ranch house. Webb and the hawks would have already been in bed except they'd had to work on the goat pen again. The goat had not quieted down after his unusually boisterous day. They discovered the weakened fence where he'd been bashing at it and repaired it while the goat was still inside. Now they were ready for bed, but the pounding of the cowboys' horses sent them to the door instead.

Webb's first thought was that Ronsey had decided on an attack. But then he recognized the riders and heard the news that the herd had been stolen again. It took only a few minutes for all the hawks to get their horses saddled and they rode out, arguing about where to try to cut off the thieves. Gilmore and Oldham expected them to turn east to the main valley again; Brill and Fleming were sure they wouldn't go back to the same spot where they had been caught before.

The decision was to go to the bedding grounds and follow the trail. They were amazed at the clarity of that trail. It seemed as if the thieves wanted to be followed. At the edge of the sand-hills, Webb halted the men. Instead of following, they would split, each group watching for signs that the herd had turned. If they could get ahead of the herd, they would stampede it back the way it had come.

They were close enough behind the herd to know they could overtake it. Cattle couldn't move as fast as horses and a herd was a difficult thing to hurry. The men divided, four curving to the east and north to get around the herd and cut it off if it did turn east; the other three curved to the west and north.

Webb went with the east group, but they found that the herd didn't turn. They were aware of the herd to their left as they passed it. Once ahead, they veered to their left to head it off. They met the group that had gone to the west. They sat quietly in their saddles, waiting for the cattle, which they could hear approaching.

The one man riding point didn't see them until he was fairly close. Webb gave the signal, and they charged forward, firing their guns in the air. Webb was sure Oldham, at least, had fired to hit the point rider. But the man had already wheeled his horse and was racing back, right into the cattle. He would have made a very difficult target to hit.

The cattle, faced with this sudden eruption of gunfire directly in their faces, wheeled and bolted back the way they had come. Webb and the hawks kept on their heels, but the cattle soon began to slow. They were not wild and the panic that had seized them soon began to wear off.

Webb wheeled wide to get around the herd. Up there in what was now the front of the herd must be the rustlers who had been driving the animals. He wanted to capture at least one of them to prove it was Ronsey's men doing the rustling.

The cattle wound around the sandhills, keeping to the valleys where the running was easier. By cutting around to the left of a hill when the cattle had bypassed on the right, Webb got up even with the leaders.

He was looking ahead for the rustlers, but hadn't seen any. They had probably cut to one side to avoid the stampede, he thought.

Then he did see a rider out in front of the herd. He urged his horse faster. He wanted to catch that man. Then he saw the horse stumble, and a chill ran over him. He hated to see anyone, even a rustler, trampled by a stampede.

The chill suddenly became ice in his middle as he got close enough to see that the rider was not one of the rustlers. It was Peggy and by no stretch of his imagination could he picture Peggy as a cattle rustler.

Her horse stumbled again and Webb could see that this time it was going down. He shot a glance back at the cattle. They weren't running with mad abandon as they had when they started, but they were still coming at a good pace. They'd likely run over anything in their path.

He spurred his horse into a dead run. He had to get to Peggy before the cattle did.

Peggy was thrown clear of the saddle, and she and the horse both got up instantly. Peggy still had a grip on the reins of her horse, but the horse had panicked when he fell and now, facing the oncoming cattle, he jerked back and stripped the reins from Peggy's hands.

Suddenly Webb was there and he wheeled his horse between Peggy and the cattle. His horse was gripped with the same panic as Peggy's horse, but Webb held an iron grip on the reins, forcing him to stop in front of the cattle.

Reaching down with one hand, Webb clutched Peggy's hand and pulled her up behind his saddle. Peggy made anything but a graceful landing, but she wrapped her arms around Webb's waist and hung on tightly.

Webb whipped off his hat and waved it frantically at the cattle bearing down on him, whooping loudly at the same time. He knew if they didn't turn aside, the cattle in the rear would force the front runners right over them.

The commotion had the desired effect. The cattle snorted in renewed fear and pushed to either side to avoid that frightening apparition. The herd split and roared by. While it seemed an eternity before the last of the cattle had passed, Webb knew it had been only a couple of minutes.

He turned in behind the herd while Peggy explained why she was out there. She told him about the ambush set for him and the hawks. There was no sign of it as the hawks drove the herd back to their pasture. Apparently the stampede had driven out the ambushers, too.

The cattle had quieted down to a slow walk by the time they were back on their pasture.

Before they left the herd, the men gathered to speculate on the next move made by the enemy. Webb was sorry he hadn't caught any of the rustlers. But what Peggy had told him about the ambush proved beyond doubt that they were Ronsey's men.

"I don't think they'll try the herd again," Webb said. "They'll come right after us now. We'd better prepare for that."

"I'd as soon go after them," Gilmore said. "Then we can pick the place and time for the fight."

"Maybe we will," Webb agreed. "But they might hit us yet tonight if they can regroup fast enough."

"We'll give them the battle of their lives wherever or whenever they strike," Brill said. "I ain't got nothing to live for but this ranch, and the only way they're going to take it from me is to kill me."

"My sentiments exactly," Oldham said.

Gilmore and Fleming nodded. Webb turned to look at Peggy and saw the surprise in her face. She hadn't seen the full extent of the determination in these men before.

"Let's go home," Webb said. "If we have company, we want to be there to greet them." He turned to King and Masters. "You boys can handle the cattle now, can't you?"

"Sure," Ike King said. "They'll be real quiet after that run."

Webb led the way to the ranch house. It was nearing midnight now. He told Peggy he'd take her home or she could stay at the ranch if she chose.

"If you've got a room for me, I'll stay," she said. "I don't want to take one of your horses. You might need every one. And I'm dog tired."

Webb knew it would be dangerous for Peggy to be out on the road tonight after Ronsey's men had taken such a setback, and it could be disastrous for any of the hawks to be caught taking her back.

He was amazed the next morning to find Peggy getting breakfast, with Lon Fleming sitting back like a king admiring her work. Webb also appreciated the breakfast. Fleming was a good cook, but he was no match for Peggy.

Before the meal was over, a rider came in. The hawks were at the front of the house waiting, guns ready. But they holstered their guns when they saw that it was Fad Vernon.

"Something wrong?" Webb asked, moving out to the hitchrack.

"Got a message for you," Fad said. "Dude Ronsey wants to see you. Something about a truce." Then his face lit up as he saw Peggy in the doorway. "Boy, I'm glad to see you. Me and your folks been worrying about you all this morning."

"I'm fine. How's Pa?"

Fad shrugged. "All right. Any reason he shouldn't be?"

Peggy sighed. "I guess not." She turned to Webb. "Do you believe Dude wants a truce?"

"He wants my hide," Webb said. "But I'll go in and see."

"Wouldn't advise it," Gilmore said quickly.

"It ain't like Dude to ask for a truce of any kind," Fad added.

"I know Dude has assigned Kurt Sikman to kill you," Peggy said.

Webb nodded. He turned to Fad. "You go on back to town. But don't tell him I'm coming. Let him guess."

"You be careful," Fad warned and turned his horse back toward him.

In half an hour, Webb saddled his horse and another for Peggy. They rode into Target, Webb leading the way in behind the store, where those up the street wouldn't be likely to see them. He didn't want anyone to know that Peggy had come in with him.

After the excited greetings between Peggy and her parents and the assurance that everyone was in fine shape, Webb reined his horse out to the south and came in on the road as if he'd just ridden in from the ranch. He reined in at the general store and went inside.

"Why'd you do that?" Peggy demanded when he got inside.

"I'm ready to let them know I'm here," Webb said. "If Sikman wants me, he's going to have to come down here after me. The odds won't all be in his favor then."

The Curetons were still exchanging stories of their own worries. Peggy's horse had come in during the night and, until Fad returned from the ranch, they'd had no idea what had happened to her. She asked how her father had escaped the stampede and he explained that, when the front of the herd wheeled back on the rest, all the riders had recognized what was coming and rode to one side and let the cattle go.

Fad came running down the street from the saloon. Coming into the store, he looked for Webb.

"They're waiting for you up at the saloon," he said. "They told me to tell you."

"All right," Webb said. "You've told me. Now go back and tell them if they want to see me, they know where I am."

Fad nodded. "I'll tell them. But you be careful. There's a lot of them and they're tricky."

"I'll take care," Webb said.

The wait dragged on for almost an hour. Webb had about decided to ride on back to the ranch when he saw Sikman dodge out the rear door of the saloon and come down toward the back of the hardware store.

"Remember what Fad said," Peggy said softly, close to Webb. "They're tricky."

Clint nodded, trying to follow Sikman's progress behind the sheds and barn between the saloon and the hardware store. He didn't see how they could pull any tricks with Sikman coming alone after him. But once the man got behind the hardware store, he didn't reappear.

Webb pushed up close to the window to watch, but he couldn't see some areas, so he stepped to the door to get a better look. That was when the rifle roared from the saloon. The bullet missed Webb by inches, and he ducked back inside.

"I see what you mean by trickery," he said. "If Sikman wants to see me, he can just come over here."

"I'm going to take a shot at the saloon," Peggy

said. "Maybe I can make whoever is shooting from there keep his head down."

Webb nodded. "They'll think I'm doing it," he said. "But that's dangerous. Be careful. I'll slip outside in case Sikman decides to get closer while he thinks I'm shooting at the saloon."

Peggy grabbed a rifle. Her father objected but not too strongly. Opening a window on the side of the store near the front of the building, Peggy poked the rifle out and fired at the window in the saloon. An answering shot came quickly, but Peggy had already ducked away from the window.

As she snapped another shot at the saloon, Webb dodged out the back door of the store. Moving quickly along the side of the store toward the front, he came to the corner where he could see the hardware store. Sikman was stealing along the side of that establishment.

Webb stepped away from the store in plain sight of Sikman but not in sight of the saloon.

"That's far enough, Sikman," he yelled.

Sikman jumped as if he'd been branded with a hot iron. Wheeling to face Webb, he stared for an instant. Webb waited. He wouldn't fight a man who wouldn't fight back.

"You—you tricked me!" Sikman screamed.

Webb knew what he meant. "You had a rifleman waiting for me. Now run or try to do what your boss told you to."

Webb could see that Sikman was shaken.

Apparently he had expected the rifleman to kill Webb or at least wound him. When that failed, he had waited until he thought Webb was involved in a shootout with the man at the saloon to try to sneak up to the store. Now he found himself facing a healthy opponent. Webb thought the coward was going to run.

Instead, with a squall like a frightened cat, Sikman swung his gun around at Webb and fired, not taking time to aim. The bullet was closer than Webb liked, snapping past his head.

Webb fired three times. Sikman answered one of those shots, but it came as he was going down and it plowed into the dirt in the middle of the street.

Webb waited to make sure the battle was over. Then he went back to the rear door and into the store. Peggy had given up the rifle battle and come to the front of the store. Sid Cureton was staring across the street at the sprawled-out body of Kurt Sikman.

"You got him," was all he said, as if he didn't believe it.

"Who'll come after me next?" Webb asked.

Nobody answered for a moment. Then Peggy said, "Quince Tucker is the only killer Dude has left now. He's very good with a gun."

"I guess I found out about the truce Ronsey wanted to discuss," Webb said. "I'll head back to the ranch now."

Peggy went outside and led Webb's horse around to the back and Webb rode toward the ranch. He met an angry crew there. Gilmore made it plain that the hawks were not going to be left out of another fight.

"How good are you with a gun, Bruce?" Webb asked Brill.

"Not as good as with a whip," Brill said. "But I'll hold my own in a fight."

"Maybe not with Tucker," Webb said. "He's after your hide for the way you whipped him. I think he murdered my parents. So let me have the first try at him."

"I figure Ronsey will gather all the men he's got and come after us," Gilmore said. "We'd better not worry about any single one of them—just the whole bunch."

Webb nodded. "Probably so. Maybe we can surprise them by taking the fight to them. We don't want to hit the Curetons. And I think Pinburg would be a decent sort of person if he wasn't bossed by Ronsey. If we can hit the north end of town where the saloon is, we should keep the fighting away from Cureton and Pinburg."

"Ronsey is short of gunmen now that Tullie Cureton and Sikman are both gone," Oldham said. "I say we ought to hit them right now."

"To surprise them, it would be best to strike about dawn, like the Indians do," Gilmore said.

“A man who’s been rousted out of sleep ain’t worth much for a while.”

They continued with their plans well into the evening. It was long after dark when Webb smelled smoke. He ran to the front of the house to discover that a fire had been started at an outside corner.

No one had to tell him who had set the fire. Nor did he need to be told that, the minute someone stepped outside to douse water on that fire, he would be shot.

Ronsey had them trapped.

XIV

"Caught like rats in a trap," Gilmore exploded.

"We can get out the back," Oldham said. "But who's going to put out the fire?"

"Let's show them what we're made of," Brill suggested. "We'll fire a few shots out there and get them to shoot at us so we can see where they are. Then we'll go out the back way and charge them."

That was about what Webb would expect from the hawks, especially Bruce Brill. He would face death rather than give up the ranch. The others seemed to agree.

"Let's try it," Webb said.

He moved to a window in the front of the house and pulled it open. The others did the same. They started up with several shots.

As Brill had predicted, there were a dozen answering shots from out in the dark beyond the fire.

"Now we know where they are," Brill said. "Let's go."

Webb led the way to the back of the house and through the rear door. He half expected someone to be watching the back door, but no shots came from the dark. Once outside, they moved up the dark side of the house to the front corner.

"We have to do what we're going to do fast," Webb said. "If we don't put out that fire soon, it'll get away from us."

"Who ain't ready?" Brill asked. "Let's go."

Webb and Brill led the charge from the corner of the house. Oldham and Gilmore filled the gap between them, with Fleming a step behind.

It was obvious from the second they hit the yard with guns blazing that the men out front were taken entirely by surprise. They might have expected almost anything but not a charge like an infantry battalion. Wild shots came from the dark, but Webb doubted if they could get very close to their targets. Their own shooting at invisible objects was little better. They had only the flashes of guns as targets.

They were halfway across the yard when Webb was aware that Oldham was staggering. Jay went down, but nobody slowed in the charge. The guns in front suddenly changed positions as Ronsey's men began running back into the darkness.

Webb and the other three hawks kept shooting until their guns were empty. Then they stopped and turned back. But there were no shots coming at them anymore. Webb heard horses running.

"Guess we licked them," Gilmore said with satisfaction. "Now let's see how bad Jay is hit."

"Got to put out the fire," Webb said.

He ran to get buckets out of the house. Fleming was right at his side. They ran to the tank that was always full of water for the cattle and horses.

Brill joined them and, in a matter of a few minutes, they had the fire out with little structural damage to the house. Gilmore was still out in the yard where Jay Oldham had fallen.

Webb hurried over there once the fire was out. He found Gilmore hunched over, his shoulders shaking.

"Is he dead?" Webb asked softly.

Gilmore nodded his head. "We got to be pretty good friends. I hope we got some of them skunks."

Webb helped Gilmore carry Oldham's body inside the house. Then Webb lit a lantern, and the two of them went out to survey the rest of the yard where the attackers had been. Webb was surprised to find two dead men there and a patch of blood at another spot, indicating that another one had been hit. For a dark night, the marksmanship of the hawks had been fantastic.

Webb examined the two dead men, but he didn't know either of them. He had hoped that one of them might be Quince Tucker, but he imagined Tucker and Ronsey had kept far back out of revolver range, if they were even here. Ronsey might have sent his cowboys on this mission without risking his own neck or that of his bodyguard.

The goat was racing around his little pen and butting anything he came to. Fleming went out with the lantern and talked to the goat. The excitement of a battle in which he couldn't take any part had been more than the goat could stand.

"Should have let Dynamite clean them out," Fleming said when he got back to the house. "He was trying his best to get in on the action."

"Maybe he smelled Dude Ronsey out there," Brill said. "Peggy says that Ronsey teased him a lot. I never heard of a goat with much of a memory, but it seems that goat never forgets anyone he has a grudge against."

Their plan to strike at Ronsey at dawn had been destroyed by the attack on the ranch and the death of Oldham. Before they headed for bed, only one mention was made of those plans and that was to cancel them. The men took turns sitting up with the body.

At dawn, Fleming started cooking breakfast. The others were up before he had it ready.

"We'll take Jay in to Norm Pinburg this morning," Webb said. "He has some caskets on hand. We'll bury him in the cemetery, but we'll have to keep an eye on Ronsey and his men. They might not respect a funeral."

They didn't hurry since hurrying didn't seem appropriate for the occasion. The sun was well up in the sky before they were ready to get the horses hitched to the wagon.

Webb had stepped out into the yard to cross to the barn when he saw a rider coming from town.

After last night's raid, he was cautious about any rider approaching the ranch. But this one was riding in boldly, not like someone on nefarious business.

He watched until he recognized Peggy. He wondered what could be bringing her out this early in the morning. The way things had been going, he couldn't expect any good news.

Peggy rode up to the hitchrack and dismounted. Webb was waiting for her.

"Something wrong?" he asked.

"There isn't much that's right," she said. "Early last evening when Pa went up to the saloon, he heard Dude tell Quince that, if things didn't work the way they planned, Quince was to lay an ambush to kill you somewhere between here and town."

Webb wasn't surprised. "What time did he hear that?" he asked.

"Before supper," Peggy said. "I don't know what Dude was hoping would turn out the way they planned."

"We know," Webb said. "They raided us last night. Set fire to the house, then waited for us to come out."

"The house doesn't look burned," Peggy said, eyes flashing over the place. Then she saw the black corner and the burned kindling where the fire had been laid. "How'd you get it out so quick?"

"We went out the back door, then charged them. They ran like sheep. Then we put out the fire."

"Anybody get hurt?"

"Jay Oldham was killed," Webb said. "We got two of them. They're still out there where they were shot. I was just on my way to get the team and wagon to take the bodies in to Pinburg."

"Jay killed?" Her voice almost broke. "Anybody else hurt?"

Webb shook his head. "I imagine this wasn't just what Ronsey wanted to happen. He lost two men and at least one hurt. And he didn't get rid of all of us. Now what about this ambush?"

"All I know is what Pa told me. We thought you ought to know so you'd be on the watch in case you went to town today."

"We have to go to town to have the funeral," Webb said. "I'll ride out and take a look. There isn't much of a hiding place between here and town where a man can lay an ambush."

"He may try to sneak in close to the ranch," Peggy said. "Or he might wait till you get in town and ambush you there. He might even try to hide in a buffalo wallow between here and town."

Webb nodded. "A buffalo wallow would make a perfect spot for an ambush. He could lie down out of sight but still see for a half mile in any direction. I'm going to ride out toward town and see what places I should avoid."

Noticing Gilmore and Brill in the doorway,

Peggy went to them while Webb headed for the corral. He'd been planning to harness the team, but instead he saddled his riding horse. It didn't take him long to ride out a mile and a half, examining the terrain and deciding just where an ambush might take place. If he moved in a zigzag fashion, he could avoid coming close to any of the buffalo wallows. Some of those wallows were particularly deep where the buffalo had rolled hard in the dust to get rid of the insects bothering them. After a rain they coated themselves with mud in those wallows. It didn't take the huge animals long to dig quite a large pit.

Webb rode back to the house, sure that he could take the wagon to town without running into an ambush. He thought he might meet Peggy going back to town, but he saw her horse still standing at the hitchrack. Likely she was in the house trying to comfort the hawks over their loss. He was sure she was as upset over Oldham's death as his partners were.

Webb had started toward the barn to put his horse away when he saw Peggy at the hitchrack, obviously waiting for him. He changed his direction and rode to the hitchrack.

"Find anything?" she asked.

"Nothing but buffalo wallows," Webb said. "I can zigzag around them and get to town all right. Are you going back home now?"

"I want to talk to you first. I brought my locket so you could look at it."

"Good." He swung out of the saddle. "I've been close to it a couple of times, but something happened each time, so I didn't get to examine it. Have you checked it?"

She nodded. "I found a picture in it. I think it's your pa, taken when he was younger than I knew him."

"Nothing else?"

She shook her head. "I even pried the picture out to see what was behind it. But there wasn't anything."

Webb's hopes faded. Maybe there wasn't any secret, after all. Or maybe Quince Tucker or Dude Ronsey had gotten to it first. Webb wished his mother had told him what the secret was.

Peggy fished a small bundle out of her saddlebag. Unwrapping it, she revealed the locket and handed it to Clint.

He took it almost reverently. He couldn't remember his mother without this locket around her neck. She didn't wear it just on Sunday; she wore it all the time.

"What do you think is in it?" Peggy asked.

"I have no idea. My mother said there was a secret there that she didn't want me to know as long as she was alive. I thought that, when I found the locket, I'd find the killer. That didn't work out."

"Pa got it from Quince Tucker. Does that mean you think Quince killed her?"

"He's the most likely suspect, don't you think?"

Peggy nodded. "But why would he kill her?"

"I don't know," Webb said. "Maybe just carrying out Ronsey's orders."

Webb led the way to the step in front of the porch. They sat down together and Webb snapped open the locket. The picture that met his eyes was indeed his father as a young man. Webb barely remembered when he had looked like that.

Carefully he pried out the picture. Peggy was right again. There was nothing behind the picture but the case of the locket. Webb turned the picture over, hoping there might be a message there. It was blank.

He turned the locket over in his hands. There were no marks on the outside other than wear. He looked inside again. It was then that he saw the tiny catch in the back of the case.

"There must be another compartment behind this," he said, showing Peggy the tiny hook.

Webb fumbled with the hook, trying to use his fingernails to open it. He gave the locket to Peggy to see if she could catch the tiny latch. She had no better luck than he'd had.

Webb dug out his knife. Carefully, he fixed the point of the blade in the tiny hook. Almost the entire back of the case opened up, revealing a thin compartment that would never have been noticeable to a casual glance.

Flattened in the compartment was a thin piece of paper, folded twice. Webb carefully pried it out with his knife. It had been there a long time. The side next to the cover was rubbed a little. But Webb couldn't see any writing on that.

Carefully, he unfolded the paper. The writing inside was his mother's. He'd know it anywhere. Inside the folds, the writing had not faded.

"Clint . . . When you read this, I'll be dead. Clarence 'Dude' Ronsey is my brother. He wanted all the inheritance. When I got half, he swore he would get my half, too. I'm afraid he'll kill me to get it. He'll kill you, too, if you claim your inheritance. Be careful. There is no hate like a family hate . . . Mother."

Webb stared at the paper in disbelief. Then he handed it to Peggy to read. She gasped as she read.

"So you think Dude killed your mother and dad?" she asked gently.

"Either he did or he had Tucker do it. This is the evidence I needed. I heard my pa speak about my mother's brother once. He said they had disowned him. He was not to be mentioned in our house again. I never guessed it was Dude Ronsey."

"What are you going to do?" Peggy asked. "You can't fight your own uncle."

"I'm not claiming him as an uncle. To me, he's the murderer of my mother. It may have been Tucker who did the killing, but Ronsey was behind it."

Webb shut the secret compartment in the locket and handed it back to her.

She shook her head. "You should have that. It was your mother's."

"It's your locket," Webb said. "Even if it was mine, nothing would please me more than to have you wear it."

Her cheeks tinged pink and she took the locket. "Thank you," she said softly.

He went back to the hitchrack with her and helped her mount. Then he turned toward the house as Peggy rode off to town.

"Peggy said that Tucker was planning to set an ambush for you," Brill said. "Did you find the spot you think he'll use?"

"Could be one of the buffalo wallows along the road," Webb said. "But we can avoid those wallows."

"We told Peggy to tell Pinburg we'll be bringing in Jay for burial," Gilmore said. "So any time we go, things should be ready."

None of them were eager to make the trip, but it was something that had to be done. Webb took some time to sort out his thinking in light of the note his mother had written. He didn't even like to think that Dude Ronsey was his uncle. And he had murdered Webb's parents, one way or another. Webb's heart filled with hatred, but he tried to keep it down. There was work to be done, and anger wouldn't help him to do it.

Finally he headed for the door. "Keep an eye on the road toward town," Webb advised the others. "I'll harness the horses. If you see any movement out there, pinpoint it so we can avoid that spot. It could be Tucker."

Leading his saddle pony to the barn, he went inside and unsaddled him. The two horses he would hitch to the wagon were out in the corral. He'd bring them into the barn to harness them.

He stepped through the back door. That was the moment Quince Tucker lunged at him. Tucker was a couple of inches taller than Webb and seventy pounds heavier.

Webb was caught completely by surprise. He certainly hadn't expected Tucker to ambush him right here at his own barn. Tucker must have kept the barn between him and the house as he sneaked in. Webb would never have expected Tucker to try to beat him to death, either, but there was no doubt in his mind that Tucker intended to do just that. He was big enough that if he got the advantage, nothing could stop him. And he certainly had the advantage now.

XV

Webb was staggered by the force of Tucker's first blow. If it hadn't been for the barn wall where Tucker's blow slammed him, he would have gone down and probably been stomped by his adversary.

He got one leg braced and stayed on his feet, but Tucker spun around and drove a fist into his shoulder. Tucker's two hundred and fifty pounds gave him a big advantage over Webb in close-in fighting.

Webb lashed out, but there wasn't room to put any force behind his blows. Backed up against the side of the barn, he was almost helpless. When Tucker pressed in for the kill, Webb suddenly dropped down and drove himself against the bartender's legs. Surprised, Tucker retreated a step and Webb drove harder. Tucker staggered but caught himself after a few backward steps that took him out of range of Webb's lunge.

Tucker came charging back, but now Webb dodged away from the barn into the corral where there was room to maneuver. He thought that Tucker could have killed him with one gunshot, but then he realized that, with the house only a few yards away, the noise would have alerted the hawks and they'd have cut Tucker down before he could have escaped.

Webb guessed that Tucker would rather beat a man to death than shoot him, anyway. There had been pure pleasure on his face when he first caught Webb by surprise. Some of that pleasure was gone now.

Tucker charged at Webb, obviously confident he could crush him if he could catch him. Webb didn't consider himself a boxer, but he was much more agile than Tucker. He dodged away as Tucker came after him, landing a stinging blow on the bartender's jaw as he passed.

Tucker wheeled and came for Webb again. Webb dodged, almost stumbling. He caught himself and twisted to meet Tucker's next blow. He knew that if he ever went down, he'd never get up.

Webb ducked under Tucker's wild swing and buried a fist in his soft paunch. Breath whistled out of him. The bodyguard stepped back, but he caught himself again and pushed forward, swinging his big fists wildly. Webb kept out of their reach. A direct blow from one of those fists could do him in.

Webb dodged another blow, then swung around and hit Tucker a vicious blow in the back. Tucker spun back to face Webb, but he didn't charge blindly this time. It was beginning to dawn on him that he wasn't going to catch Webb and beat him into the ground.

He made one more charge and Webb side-stepped it easily. Tucker was playing out. Sensing that he could beat the big man, Webb started forward. But when Tucker turned this time, he was drawing his gun.

Webb threw himself sideways, grabbing his own gun. Tucker's weapon roared and the bullet cut the air where Webb had been an instant before. Webb quickly fired. He knew he had missed.

Tucker, apparently panicking now that Webb had his gun in action, fired twice more. One bullet cut a chunk out of Webb's sleeve and dug a little furrow in his arm. The other was a complete miss.

Tucker was too weary to hold his gun steady. Webb was tired, too. Throwing his left hand under his right arm for a brace, Webb held his weary hand steady and fired once more just as Tucker fired a fourth time. Again Tucker missed, but Webb didn't. Tucker collapsed in the corral dust.

Webb moved cautiously toward Tucker, who still gripped his gun. The man didn't make a move and Webb kicked the gun away. He saw then that Tucker wasn't dead.

Leaning down, Webb asked the one question he wanted answered. "Did you kill my mother and father?"

Tucker glared at him, but the knowledge that it made no difference now was in his eyes. "Dude made me do it," he whispered.

Tucker shuddered and was still. Webb checked his pulse. There was none. He straightened up just as Bruce Brill burst through the barn into the corral.

"We heard the shooting. What in blazes—" He saw Tucker's body then. "You got him," he gasped.

"He almost got me," Webb said, leaning wearily against the barn.

"We'd have been right out here to help if we'd known," Brill said.

Gilmore and Fleming came running through the barn then. Webb explained what had happened.

"Ronsey doesn't have anybody to shield him now," Fleming said, rubbing his chin. "He had Tullie Cureton and Sikman and Tucker. Now they're all dead. Think he'll give up and get out?"

Webb thought of his mother's note. Ronsey wanted all of his sister's inheritance. That inheritance had apparently set up and stocked this ranch for the Webbs.

"I think he'll still try to kill us all off," Webb said. "He wants this ranch. He has just what he wants here in this rustling setup, but he can't keep it unless he gets rid of us."

"We have enough dead men around here to start a cemetery," Gilmore said. "How many should we take in to the hardware man to fit for coffins?"

"Just our own," Webb said. "We'll let Pinburg come out and pick up the others."

They carried Tucker to the front of the barn and Webb went back to hitch the team. The horses had been excited by the shooting and were hard to manage.

Fleming had gone out to the goat pen to calm down the billy goat. Webb wondered if somebody had shot at the goat. There had to be some explanation for his getting so excited every time he heard guns going off.

Webb kept thinking about the trouble they were sure to run into in town. If Ronsey saw Webb coming in—while Tucker hadn't returned—he'd know that Webb had somehow beaten Tucker. Clint was sure Ronsey would rally his men for a battle. There were only three hawks and Webb now. Ronsey could throw three times that many men against them.

"Maybe we ought to wait to see what Ronsey does before we go into town," Fleming suggested.

"We can't wait too long with these bodies," Brill said. "They have to be buried today."

Webb nodded. "You're right. I'll harness up and we'll get going."

Webb had the team harnessed, trying to think how they could avoid a confrontation with Ronsey's men, when Fleming came running into the barn.

"Company coming," he said. "Looks like an army."

Webb forgot about the horses. Maybe they weren't going to have to dodge Ronsey's men in town. The battle might be right here.

He ran to the front of the barn and looked at the road. They were coming, ten riders. Not an army but more than enough to go against the four of them.

"Must have had an agreement with Tucker that they'd come out to clean things up after he killed you," Brill said to Webb. "He'll have a little more cleaning up than he planned. Is Ronsey himself with them?"

"I think I see Ronsey right at the head of the bunch," Webb said. "He's probably the only leader they have now. Let's get into the house."

Leaving the barn, the men dodged across to the house. Webb imagined that Ronsey and his men saw them make the move. It made no difference now. There was no surprise in their attack.

Once inside the house, the men moved around the windows where they could command a view of the yard. All the windows were open, ready for action.

"We have to get two and a half apiece," Fleming said. "There's ten of them and four of us."

"Fair enough odds," Brill said. "I feel up to knocking off my share."

The men riding in stopped well out of range.

Webb watched them as Ronsey talked to them. Like a general, he sent some men one way and some the other.

"He's not going to try to charge in and run over us," Brill said.

"Probably learned last night that we fight back," Gilmore retorted.

"Looks to me like he plans to lay a siege," Webb said. "Don't make a target of yourselves trying to get a shot at one of them."

"They'll probably work in teams," Brill added. "One of them will inch out where we think we have a shot at him. When we move out to shoot, his partner will pick us off."

Some of Ronsey's men circled in behind the barn, others moved over to keep the front windows under their guns. Webb watched Dude Ronsey. Where would he place himself?

For twenty minutes not a shot was fired, but both sides were totally aware that the other side was ready to fight. Ronsey himself stayed behind the feed shed, which was at the extreme range of a six-gun. He kept one man with him, probably a messenger so he could contact his men without exposing himself.

Webb saw one man run back from the barn to the feed shed. Evidently he had seen Tucker's body and was reporting to Ronsey. Two minutes after the man got to Ronsey, guns opened up from the barn and from behind an old broken wagon to the east. The front and side of the house were well covered.

Webb fired his rifle when he thought he had a target or could come close enough to keep a man from returning the fire. But mostly he kept his eye on the feed shed. If Ronsey showed himself, he wanted to be ready to take advantage of it.

But Ronsey didn't expose himself. He was making sure that, if anybody escaped this fight unscathed, he'd be the one. Webb began to worry as the sun passed its zenith. If the siege went on till dark, Ronsey's men would likely try to burn them out of the house again. This time they'd probably do a better job than they had last night.

Webb kept thinking about Dude Ronsey. If Ronsey was taken out of the picture, the others would probably quit. The boss who paid them their wages could demand loyalty only as long as he lived to pay those wages.

"Lon," Gilmore called from the kitchen. "You're going to have to go out and calm down the goat. He's going to have a heart attack."

"Probably sees Ronsey," Brill said. "Yoder said he hated him."

Webb realized that the goat could probably see Ronsey behind the feed shed from his position in the pen. He didn't know whether that would have anything to do with the goat's nervousness. Maybe it was just the shooting that the goat didn't like. But he had seen the way Dynamite had singled out those who had tormented him when they had turned him into the saloon. He must have a special hatred for certain people.

Clint moved over into the kitchen where he could see the goat. Dynamite was racing around the pen, rearing up on his back legs and ramming the fence every few seconds.

Webb studied the yard between him and the goat pen. Could he make it out there to release the goat? The goat might just go crazy and leave the country. And he might head for Ronsey. That would flush him out from behind the feed bin, and they could get a shot at him.

Webb slipped over to a side window and crawled through. Nobody could see him there, but when he moved away from the house toward the goat pen, he'd be in plain sight of anybody in the barn.

He moved to the corner of the house and peered around. Taking one step away from the house, he stopped. A shot roared from the barn and wood splintered from the corner of the house.

It was enough to convince Webb. He turned and crawled back through the window into the kitchen.

"That was a fool move to make," Gilmore said.

"Had to find out," Webb said. "They're watching." He studied the pen where the goat was. Then he leveled the rifle out the window.

"You're not going to shoot the goat, are you?" Gilmore demanded.

"Got a better idea," Webb said. "If I'm a good enough shot."

Carefully he aimed and fired. The latch on the goat pen jumped but didn't break. Webb levered another shell into the barrel and aimed again. This time the latch fell away.

Webb moved back from the window to watch. The goat was even more excited than before. Rearing on his hind legs, he rammed the fence again. The second time he did that, he hit the gate and it popped open.

The goat didn't waste a second figuring out how he happened to be free. He took off like a white streak straight for the feed shed. A wild shot came his way and then the goat was at the shed. Ronsey's scream could be heard all over the yard.

"Kill that goat!"

Ronsey broke out from behind the shed with the goat only a jump behind. He shouted his order again and the men began shooting at the goat. The goat didn't appear to be hit, but one bullet caught Ronsey in midstride. He went down and was still.

The guns went silent. With Ronsey down, killed by his own men, the fight faded out of the others. Webb told the hawks to hold their fire and see what happened.

The goat ran up to Ronsey. But when he didn't move, Dynamite stalked away as if it was below his dignity to fight something that didn't run or fight back.

The men from the barn retreated and moved out to their horses. They met the men from the other side. They swung into the saddles and turned their mounts toward town.

"That takes care of that," Brill said. "Now we've got another body for Pinburg to come and get. Let's get Jay's body into town and bury it."

Webb agreed. He wouldn't be afraid of any interference if they went to town now. He went to the barn and got the horses that he had harnessed before the raiders arrived.

Fleming drove the wagon while the other three were on horseback and rode along as an escort. The town looked deserted when they came in sight of it. They drove up to the hardware store and called Norm Pinburg out, explaining what they needed.

While Fleming and Gilmore took care of the arrangements, Brill called Webb aside. "Me and the boys talked it over while you were getting the horses out of the barn. We decided we'd move out to the bunkhouse now and live there."

"Why?" Webb exclaimed. "Don't you like my company?"

"Not as much as a certain girl we know. We

saw how you looked at her. But, more important, we saw how she looked at you."

"Hey, you're jumping at wild conclusions," Webb said.

"Just logical conclusions," Brill said, grinning. "That ranch has to have a woman. We can't keep it a bachelor's den."

Webb was trying to think of a way to cut down Brill's unbridled speculations when he saw Peggy coming out of the general store and crossing the street to them.

"Dude's men rode into town a few minutes ago," she said. "Got their things and rode out again. Didn't say a word to anybody. What happened?"

"They tried to lay a siege on the ranch. But Dynamite got out and made a run at Ronsey. He yelled for his men to shoot the goat and then he got in the way of one of the bullets himself."

"Oh," she said. "What about Dynamite?"

"Didn't get a scratch that we could see. But he sure saved us a dirty job of getting rid of Ronsey."

"We can breathe free again," Peggy said. "We don't know how to thank you."

"You can thank Dynamite," Webb said. He paused. Brill had gone on into the hardware store with the other hawks. "Bruce says he and the boys are moving out into the bunkhouse on the ranch. It's going to get mighty lonesome in that big house all by myself."

“What are you going to do about it?” she asked, eyes twinkling.

Webb realized that Brill had seen things with clearer eyes than he had. He reached out and pulled her to him. “How about this?” he asked, kissing her warmly.

She smiled up at him. “It’s a good start.”

Center Point Large Print
600 Brooks Road / PO Box 1
Thorndike, ME 04986-0001 USA

(207) 568-3717

US & Canada:
1 800 929-9108
www.centerpointlargeprint.com